FATE'S TALE

A DANCE OF DEATH

BY R.O. LANDO

DORRANCE
PUBLISHING CO
EST. 1920
PITTSBURGH, PENNSYLVANIA 15238

Dorrance Publishing Co
585 Alpha Drive
Pittsburgh, PA 15238
Visit our website at *www.dorrancebookstore.com*

ISBN: 979-8-89127-574-4
eISBN: 979-8-89127-072-5

FATE'S TALE

A DANCE OF DEATH

"Time may grant us moments of respite, but Death lingers, patiently awaiting its rightful turn, for its arrival cannot be evaded, only delayed."

Table of Contents

Chapter One

A Spanish Escape

Amelia gazed out of the small airplane window, her eyes sparkling with anticipation. The sun-drenched landscape below unfolded like a vibrant tapestry, inviting her into a world of new adventures. She adjusted her seatbelt and turned to her boyfriend, Carlos, who sat beside her with a contagious grin on his face.

Carlos, with his tousled dark hair and warm brown eyes, radiated a sense of adventure. He was her partner in crime, her pillar of support, and the one who always pushed her to step out of her comfort zone. And today was no exception.

The couple had been planning their dream vacation to Spain for months. From the moment Amelia had laid eyes on photos of Barcelona's awe-inspiring architecture, Madrid's bustling streets, and the picturesque beaches of Costa del Sol, she knew this trip would be an experience like no other.

The hum of the engines filled the cabin as the plane soared through the sky, bridging the gap between their everyday lives and the enchanting world that awaited them.

Amelia's mind drifted to the countless memories they would create together—a story of laughter, exploration, and cultural immersion.

As the plane leveled off, the flight attendant's voice crackled over the intercom, announcing their impending descent into the bustling city of Barcelona. Amelia's heart fluttered with excitement, and she squeezed Carlos's hand, their fingers intertwining in a gesture of shared anticipation.

The plane gently touched down on the runway, and the couple disembarked, joining the throngs of travelers making their way through the bustling airport. Amelia couldn't help but notice the vibrant energy in the air, the distinct blend of languages filling her ears, and the tantalizing aroma of freshly brewed coffee wafting through the terminal.

With their luggage in tow, Amelia and Carlos stepped outside into the warm Spanish sunshine. The city greeted them with open arms, its streets alive with the rhythmic pulse of life. The sound of clinking glasses, lively conversations, and flamenco music filled the air, beckoning them to immerse themselves in the vibrant portrait of Spanish culture.

Amelia's eyes sparkled with a mixture of wonder and excitement as she turned to Carlos. "Can you believe we're finally here?" she exclaimed, her voice filled with awe.

Carlos grinned and pulled her into a tight embrace. "I knew this trip would be unforgettable," he said, his voice filled with warmth. "And with you by my side, Amelia, it's going to be a thousand times better."

Amelia's heart swelled with love for the man standing before her. In that moment, she knew that this Spanish adventure would not only be about exploring a new country but also about discovering the depths of their own relationship.

Hand in hand, Amelia and Carlos set off, ready to embark on an extraordinary journey—a journey that would weave their souls into the vibrant fabric of Spain, forever etching their love story into the hearts of those they encountered along the way.

Unbeknownst to them, a hooded figure lurked just beyond their peripheral vision, hidden amidst the bustling crowd. From the moment Amelia and Carlos had stepped off the plane, this mysterious presence had been watching their every move, an observer in the shadows._

Chapter Two

A DEADLY PURCHASE

Amelia and Carlos strolled hand in hand through the bustling Spanish market. The air was filled with vibrant colors, savory scents, and the lively chatter of the locals. It was a perfect day to explore, and their excitement was palpable.

As they weaved through the market stalls, a particularly boisterous salesman caught Carlos's attention. Curious about the commotion, he turned to see what was going on, leaving Amelia momentarily unattended.

Unbeknownst to him, Amelia's gaze was momentarily drawn away from Carlos, lured by a haunting yet enchanting tune that seemed to echo through the air. The melody whispered to her, beckoning her to follow its trail and discover its source. Feeling a magnetic pull, Amelia let go of Carlos's hand, her curiosity getting the better of her.

She meandered through the market, weaving between vendors and shoppers until she found herself in a secluded corner. There, beneath a faded red umbrella, stood a weathered wooden table, toppled with a chaotic collection of eccentric knick-knacks and peculiar devices. At the helm of the table, a mysterious figure dressed in a hooded cloak tended to the odd treasures.

Amelia's gaze fixated on a beautiful miniature music box, intricately adorned with delicate carvings of flowers and leaves. Its polished mahogany surface gleamed under the dappled sunlight, and the enchanting tune seemed to emanate from its delicate mechanism. Transfixed, Amelia stepped closer, her heart pounding with anticipation.

The hooded figure, sensing her presence, looked up, revealing a pair of piercing, knowing eyes. "Ah, señorita." The figure spoke in a voice that resonated with age and wisdom. "You have found your way to me."

Amelia's voice trembled as she asked, "What is this music box? It's unlike anything I've ever seen before."

The hooded figure smiled, revealing a glimpse of a weathered face beneath the cloak. "It is more than just a music box, my dear," he replied. "It holds within it the memories of forgotten stories and the whispers of distant lands. It is a vessel of magic and wonder."

Amelia's heart swelled with intrigue. She felt an inexplicable connection to the music box as if it held a piece of her own story. Without hesitation, she reached into her bag, pulled out a handful of coins, and placed them on the table.

The hooded figure nodded and accepted her payment, sliding the music box gently across the table.

As Amelia reached out to pick up the music box, dark gray clouds began to roll in. The sky began to crash with lightning and thunder, and a harsh rain began to batter

Amelia. Startled by the sudden change in weather she looked over to the old man to ask if she could seek shelter under his umbrella, however what she saw stopped the very air she breathed from leaving her body.

A strong gust of wind had swept across the stand, throwing the trinkets and scattering them all over the road. The umbrella was lifted in the air and sent flying, never to touch the earth again. There standing, unfazed and unhooded, was the old man, only now he had a sinister smile stretched across his face.

Terrified by his unnatural smile, Amelia stepped back. Catching her heel on a rock, she lost her balance and fell to the floor. The old man let out an insidious cackle that seemed to echo in the air. "It's been far too long since someone was worthy to play my game. To hear my song, to dance with me." As the wind grew stronger the old man's face and hands began to decay. The wind chipped away at his skin as if it were made of sand until nothing but bone remained.

Amelia sat there unable to move, paralyzed with fear. A look of shock was all she could muster as she watched the skeletal figure outstretch its arm toward her. A gurgled "Will you dance with me, Amelia?" came from the skeletal mouth of the old man. With tears streaming down her face, unable to speak, she did the only thing she could: cry. The skeletal being let out another loud cackle and began reaching closer to Amelia. With the little strength she found she quickly covered her eyes. All the while hearing its monstrous laugh and feeling his hand getting closer and closer, inch by agonizing inch. Amelia did not dare remove her hands from her eyes, she just sat there and cried, waiting for the inevitable to happen.

She then felt a hand touch her shoulder. Kicking herself back, she let out a scream. "No!" Yet nothing happened. She slowly opened her eyes and, to her surprise, there stood a woman. A look of concern and bewilderment lay on her face. Amelia looked around, the hooded figure vanished, disappearing along with all the items and the table. The weather was still perfect, with not a cloud in sight. Amelia quickly stood up, wiping the tears from her cheeks. The woman and concerned vendors continued their tasks at hand. The bustling market returned to its usual noise and liveliness as if nothing had happened at all. Confusion and disbelief filled Amelia's mind as she tried to comprehend the strange encounter.

She hurried back to Carlos, eager to share her experience, but as she recounted her encounter with Death, his response was dismissive. He thought it was nothing more than a figment of her imagination, a result of being momentarily alone in the market. Beginning to cry again, Carlos hugged her deeply. "Come on. Let's head back to the hotel," said Carlos. Holding her close, they headed back somberly, as the sun began to set behind them. Putting an end to an eventful day.

They only had one more day on their vacation before they had to head back home. "Where should we explore on our last day?" asked Carlos.

"I think I'm just gonna stay in today. I'm not feeling too good, I think I'll stay in," said Amelia. Carlos, trying to be understanding, volunteered to stay with her. "Go ahead and explore without me. Don't forget to bring me back something."

Carlos smiled. "I'll be back before you know it." And he quickly headed out the door. With Carlos gone, the hotel room seemed eerily quiet. Amelia began to grow uneasy; the slightest creeks made her jump. "Maybe a nice hot bath will help me relax." She filled her bathtub with warm water and added fragrant oils, hoping to find solace in its soothing embrace.

As she eased herself into the bath, closing her eyes, the haunting tune echoed in her mind once again. Flashes of her encounter with the hooded figure invaded her thoughts, interrupting her intended relaxation. Amelia desperately tried to forget about her experience and enjoy the little time she had left on her vacation, but all she could think of was that awful cackle, and when she closed her eyes, all she could see was that skeletal hand reaching for her.

She tried to push the disturbing images aside, focusing on the warmth enveloping her body. But as the water lapped against her skin, it seemed to carry an undertone of melancholy, mirroring the chilling melody that plagued her existence. Amelia immersed herself in the water, attempting to wash away the weight of her burden. However, with each splash and ripple, her mind conjured vivid recollections of the treacherous experience.

The water took on an ominous hue in her imagination, as if reflecting the shadows that lurked within her memories. She could almost feel the presence of the hooded figure, Death personified, watching her from the depths. Determined to find a moment of respite, Amelia closed her eyes and tried to steady her breathing. She immersed herself in the sensation of water against her skin, attempting to drown out the persistent echoes of that infernal tune. But as she relaxed further, a phantom sensation swept over her, as if she were sinking into an abyss. The music box's haunting melody swirled in her mind, intensifying with each passing moment.

Amelia's body tensed, and she found herself gasping for air, her heart pounding in her chest. The visions of the hooded figure grew more vivid, threatening to consume her fragile peace. Struggling to regain control, Amelia forced herself to open her eyes. The familiar surroundings of her bathroom greeted her, but an undeniable sense of foreboding lingered in the air.

Amelia's heart skipped a beat as a sudden knock reverberated through her apartment. Startled, she called out, "Who is it?" but received no response. Her mind raced with possibilities, the eerie encounters of the past still fresh in her memory.

With a mixture of apprehension and curiosity, she quickly wrapped herself in a bathrobe and tiptoed toward the front door. Peering through the peephole, she found emptiness on the other side. No one stood in the hotel hallway.

A surge of unease washed over her, but an inexplicable force compelled her to open the door fully. As she swung it open, her eyes darted to the ground, and there it lay—the music box, resting innocently, as if awaiting her arrival.

Amelia's hands trembled as she bent down to pick it up. The weight of the music box felt heavy in her palms, as if it held the weight of her destiny within its delicate exterior. She traced her fingers along the intricate carvings, their patterns now etched in her mind.

A mix of emotions washed over her—fear, curiosity, and a lingering thread of hope. Why had the music box returned to her? Was it a gift or a warning? She felt the presence of Death lurking in the shadows, his unseen hand guiding the course of events.

She slammed the door shut and placed the music box on the dresser. As Amelia stared at the music box, tears welled up in her eyes, finally spilling over and streaming down her cheeks. The weight of her overwhelming sense of loneliness crashed down upon her all at once.

She cried, allowing her tears to wash away the fear, frustration, and confusion that had built up inside her. The sobs wracked her body until exhaustion took over, lulling her into a deep slumber.

In the midst of her restless sleep, Amelia sensed a presence, a soft whisper that danced on the edge of her consciousness. She slowly opened her eyes, blinking away the remnants of her tears, and there stood Carlos, her ever-supportive boyfriend, by her side.

His gentle hand rested on her shoulder, offering a comforting touch that melted away her anxiety. Amelia looked into his eyes, her gaze filled with a mixture of gratitude and vulnerability. "Carlos," she whispered, her voice laced with weariness and relief. "I'm so glad you're here."

Handing her a hand-crafted wooden rose, he said, "Come on, let's go home," sensing that was all Amelia really wanted to hear. With a soft smile and tears still in her eyes, she nodded. Throwing her face to his chest, she hugged him as if it were the last time they would ever see each other again. Carlos hugged her back and, for a brief moment, he felt it too.

Amelia and Carlos nestled in each other's arms, finding solace and strength in their embrace. Their bodies molded together, seeking warmth and comfort in the darkness of the night. They refused to let go, as if their love alone could shield them from the perils that lay ahead.

Outside, the world remained quiet, the night sky giving way to a faint glimmer of dawn. The soft hues of orange and pink gently painted the horizon, signaling the arrival of a fresh beginning. It was a reminder that no matter how dark the night, the sun would always rise, bringing with it the promise of hope and renewal.

Chapter Three

A FRAGILE PEACE AND
A NIGHTMARE RETURNS

Months had passed since Amelia and Carlos returned home from their harrowing journey in Spain. Life seemed to have regained its normal rhythm, and Amelia's cheery demeanor had returned, as if the haunting experience were nothing more than a distant nightmare. Yet, deep down, she knew that the events in Spain had left an indelible mark on her soul.

One fateful night, as the city slumbered beneath a blanket of darkness, Amelia found herself caught in the clutches of a nightmare. She awoke in a cold sweat, her heart racing, the images of the past resurfacing with vivid intensity. She tried to shake off the lingering fear, attributing it to the haunting memories that still plagued her subconscious.

However, just as she began to regain her composure, a familiar voice echoed through the room. "Dance with me, Amelia." The words hung heavy in the air, sending a shiver down her spine. Amelia's gaze was drawn to the darkest corner of the room, where a vague silhouette of a hooded figure lingered, its presence suffocating.

Paralyzed by fear, Amelia's attempts to wake Carlos were futile. Desperation etched on her face, she pleaded with him to wake up, to acknowledge the menacing presence that loomed in the shadows. But her voice seemed to fall on deaf ears, further amplifying her growing terror.

As the hooded figure extended a shadowy hand toward her, Amelia screamed, piercing the silence, jolting Carlos awake. Disoriented and alarmed, he searched the room, his eyes meeting Amelia's terrified gaze. She pointed to the corner, her voice trembling as she whispered, "There's something there." Carlos cautiously rose from the bed, grabbing a baseball bat for a sense of security. Determined to protect Amelia, he made his way toward the light switch, flicking it on. Amelia shielded her eyes, momentarily overwhelmed by the sudden brightness.

When she dared to open her eyes again, the corner of the room stood empty, devoid of any sinister presence. Confusion swirled within her, the boundary between reality and nightmare blurring. Carlos, though visibly concerned, wore a perplexed expression. There was no evidence of the shadowy figure Amelia had seen. Sensing Amelia's distress, Carlos gently took her into his arms, providing comfort and reassurance. He suggested seeking professional help, urging her to consider therapy as a means to confront the residual trauma that plagued her.

Amelia hesitated, her mind grappling with the idea of seeking outside assistance. But deep down, she knew that Carlos was right. The events in Spain had left scars that could not be easily brushed aside. Perhaps a therapist could help her navigate the complexities of her experience, offering guidance and support as she confronted the shadow that lurked within.

With a mixture of apprehension and hope, Amelia nodded, grateful for Carlos's unwavering support. As the night gradually surrendered to the first light of dawn, Amelia made a silent vow to herself. She would confront the shadows, seeking solace in the guidance of a professional. The path to liberation might be fraught with challenges, but with Carlos by her side and the help of a therapist, she would find the strength to face her demons head-on.

And so, as the sun began to cast its gentle glow upon the world, Amelia embarked on a new chapter of her journey—one that would delve into the depths of the human psyche, unraveling the mysteries of the mind, and ultimately empowering her to reclaim her peace of mind.

In the days that followed, Amelia diligently researched and sought out a reputable therapist specializing in trauma and nightmares. She found Dr. Sofia Ramirez, a compassionate and experienced professional who seemed well-equipped to help her navigate the lingering effects of her haunting experience.

Amelia embarked on her first therapy session. Dr. Ramirez provided a safe space for her to share her fears, recount the events in Spain, and explore the emotional turmoil that had plagued her ever since. Through empathetic listening and gentle guidance, the therapist helped Amelia unravel the layers of her trauma, helping her understand that it was natural to experience such distressing dreams and flashbacks.

Over time, Amelia's therapy sessions proved transformative. She gained tools and coping strategies to manage her anxiety and panic attacks, gradually learning to distinguish between the echoes of the past and the present reality. Dr. Ramirez's support and expertise gave her a renewed sense of hope, reminding her that healing was possible.

Meanwhile, Carlos stood by Amelia's side, attending some sessions with her to better understand her experiences and provide his unwavering support. He learned about the intricacies of trauma, gaining insight into Amelia's journey and the importance of patience, empathy, and understanding.

As the therapy sessions progressed, Amelia's nightmares gradually subsided. The dreams of the haunting music box and the shadowy figure no longer plagued her every night. Instead, she began to dream of moments of peace, joyful experiences, and a future free from the shackles of fear.

Once again everything seemed okay, Carlos was away at work, and Amelia was at home preparing dinner. Listening to her favorite song on the speaker and dancing along while chopping some vegetables. Suddenly the song began to cut in and out, with static replacing every other word.

Amelia gasped as the cheerful melody she had been dancing to morphed into an unsettling cacophony of static and the haunting music box tune. The once vibrant room was now shrouded in an eerie atmosphere as the lights flickered, casting a disorienting shadow across the walls.

Startled by the sudden change, Amelia's hand slipped, and the knife plunged deep into her finger, causing searing pain and a gush of blood. She recoiled in agony, clutching her injured hand, as panic coursed through her veins.

The room seemed to grow darker, the music box tune echoing louder, enveloping her in its chilling grip. Fear gripped her heart as she fought to maintain her composure, desperately searching for a way to escape the nightmare that seemed to have taken hold of her once again.

With trembling hands, Amelia reached for the switch to turn off the music, but it refused to respond. The haunting tune continued to play relentlessly, its ominous notes taunting her very sanity. Each passing second felt like an eternity, the pain from her injured finger intensifying with every beat of the cursed melody. It was only when Amelia ripped the cord from the wall and smashed the speaker on the floor that the tune finally stopped. With the room silent she could finally collect her thoughts.

Summoning her courage, Amelia rushed to the sink, blood dripping from her wounded hand, determined to wash away the pain and chaos. But as she held her hand under the running water, a strange gurgling sound emanated from the drain. Her heart raced, and her breath caught in her throat, as she leaned in closer to listen. "Dance with me, Amelia," whispered a chilling voice from the depths of the drain. The words echoed in her mind, sending shivers down her spine. Unable to process what had just occurred, she stumbled backward, her feet slipping on the blood that had pooled on the floor. In an instant, everything went dark as she lost consciousness.

When Amelia regained consciousness, she found herself lying in a hospital room, the soft hum of medical equipment filling the silence. Disoriented and disheveled, she tried to piece together what had transpired, but her memory was fragmented, like shards of a broken mirror.

Carlos sat beside her, his face contorted with worry. Relief washed over her as she saw his familiar presence, but the weight of her experience and the uncertainty of her own mind weighed heavily on her. Amelia mustered the strength to explain the events that had unfolded, her voice filled with urgency and desperation. She shared the disjointed fragments of the night, the music box tune, the flickering lights, and the chilling voice from the drain. She implored Carlos to believe her, to see the terror that had once again invaded her life.

But instead of the support and understanding she expected, she was met with disbelief. Carlos's face twisted with frustration and doubt, his eyes reflecting a mixture of concern and irritation. "Amelia, this can't be real. It's all in your mind," he said with a tinge of frustration, his voice laced with disbelief. Tears welled up in Amelia's eyes as she realized that the one person she had hoped would stand by her side was slipping away, consumed by skepticism and the inability to comprehend the inexplicable. The fracture in their trust widened, leaving her feeling even more isolated and alone.

As the evening descended, casting long shadows across the hospital room, Amelia's tears flowed unabated. She felt the weight of Carlos's disbelief and departure bearing down on her, intensifying her sense of loneliness and abandonment.

Alone in the dimly lit room, Amelia clung to the thin thread of hope that had guided her thus far. She knew that her experiences were real, that there was something sinister lurking in the shadows, tormenting her with its haunting presence. But without Carlos's support, doubts began to seep into her mind, whispering that perhaps she was truly losing touch with reality.

The hospital room, once a place of healing, now felt suffocating and oppressive. Amelia longed for the comfort of familiar surroundings, for the embrace of loved ones who understood and believed her. But she was met with silence, the echo of her cries reverberating in the empty space.

It was late in the night. Amelia lay there unable to move. Her thoughts quiet, her mind empty. She no longer had tears to cry. A faint whistling coming from the room next to her snapped her out of her sad state. Amelia's eyes widened as she strained to listen to the faint sound of whistling. It was a delicate melody, haunting yet familiar. Her heart skipped a beat as recognition washed over her—it was the tune of the music box.

Amelia, recognizing the tune, began to panic, hitting the call light button. The whistling stopped. "No one is coming Amelia," a coarse voice said. As her heart began to race, she clicked the button again. "You're all alone," the voice said, letting out a small chuckle afterward. Amelia began clicking the button as fast as she could until she heard a noise that stopped her in an instant. A footstep, then another, and another, slowly making its way toward her room. "Amelia. Will you dance with me, Amelia?" Amelia was too scared to speak; she just sat there unable to move. "Oh, Amelia. Will you dance with me?"

Amelia's breath quickened, her body trembling with fear as the footsteps drew closer. The voice, dripping with an eerie mix of amusement and malice, continued to taunt her. She desperately searched for an escape, her gaze darting around the room, but the walls seemed to close in, trapping her in a nightmare.

She began to look around for anything to defend herself. "There you are," said the hooded figure now standing in her doorway. Amelia's heart pounded in her chest as the voice echoed through her room. She felt a cold sweat forming on her brow, her instincts urging her to run, to hide from the impending presence. But deep down, she knew that she couldn't escape the grasp of the supernatural force that pursued her.

As the hooded figure made its way towards her bed Amelia grabbed hold of the only thing she could, the bedside telephone. Waiting for the perfect moment to strike, until its head was within arm's reach. She struck it as hard as she could. A loud screech could be heard as it fell to the floor. Within a matter of moments, a hospital aide came into the room and flicked on the lights. "What did you do?" the aide asked. Amelia, still in shock with what happened, could not speak. As the aide ran out of the room calling for help, Amelia began to come to her senses.

Amelia's heart raced as she took in the horrifying scene before her. The weight of what had just transpired settled heavily upon her shoulders, intertwining fear and disbelief. She trembled, her hands stained with the consequences of her actions.

The hospital staff rushed into the room, their expressions a mix of shock and confusion. Amelia tried to find her voice, to explain what had occurred, but the words caught in her throat. She could barely comprehend the reality of what she had just witnessed.

The hospital staff exchanged worried glances as they tried to make sense of the chaotic scene before them. Amidst the commotion, Amelia's words fell on skeptical ears. They dismissed her claims as delusions brought on by stress or trauma. They believed that Amelia had attacked the nurse out of a fit of madness.

Amelia's heart dropped to her stomach as she watched the hooded figure, standing there with a twisted smile and a sinister aura that chilled her to the bone. The room was filled with chaos as medical staff rushed to tend to the injured nurse and restrain Amelia, oblivious to the presence that haunted her. Fear and desperation consumed Amelia as she pleaded with the staff, her voice filled with urgency. "Please, you have to believe me! There was someone here, the hooded figure! He's still here!"

But her words fell on deaf ears. The staff dismissed her claims as the delusions of a disturbed and traumatized patient. They sedated her, their intentions rooted in their belief that they were helping her. As sedatives coursed through her veins, Amelia's protests grew fainter. Her pleas for them to believe her turned into desperate whispers that went unheard. They deemed her a danger to herself and others, confining her to a room under heavy sedation.

Days turned into weeks as Amelia languished in the confines of the psychiatric ward. The whispers of the music box tune still echoed in her mind, a constant reminder of the curse that clung to her. She felt trapped, both physically and mentally, a prisoner of her own reality.

Chapter Four

R E L E A S E   A N D   R E U N I O N

A melia sat on the couch in a small office, her hands fidgeting nervously in her lap. The doctor, Dr. Roberts, observed her closely, his demeanor calm and attentive. His office walls were adorned with serene paintings and shelves filled with books, creating an atmosphere of tranquility. Dr. Roberts made a few notes on his notepad before looking up at Amelia with a gentle smile. "I'm glad to hear that you're feeling okay, Amelia. It seems like you've made significant progress since we last spoke."

Amelia nodded, her eyes darting around the room as she collected her thoughts. "Yes, things have been better lately. I've been focusing on my therapy, trying to make sense of everything that happened."

Her composure calm and collected as she spoke to Dr. Roberts. She had learned to mask her fear and anxiety, appearing as though she no longer saw the hooded figure or heard the haunting music box tune. It was a necessary facade, an attempt to convince the doctor that she was ready to be released from the psychiatric ward.

"I understand your concerns, Dr. Roberts," Amelia said, her voice steady. "I'm truly sorry for what happened to the nurse, but I assure you that I am no longer experiencing those hallucinations. I've been working hard in therapy, and I believe I have made significant progress in managing my fears and anxieties."

Dr. Roberts regarded Amelia with a careful gaze, analyzing her every word and expression. He had seen many patients who were desperate to leave the confines of the psychiatric ward, eager to regain their freedom. But his duty as a psychiatrist was to prioritize their well-being and ensure their safety.

"Amelia, I appreciate your determination and the progress you have made," Dr. Roberts replied, his voice gentle yet cautious. "However, it's essential that we proceed with caution. The events you described were deeply traumatic, and we need to ensure that you have the necessary support and coping mechanisms in place."

Amelia nodded, her eyes conveying her sincerity. "I understand, Dr. Roberts. I am committed to my therapy and continuing the work we have started. I am confident that I can manage any challenges that may arise."

Dr. Roberts leaned back in his chair, considering Amelia's words. He had seen her transformation, witnessed her resilience and growth over the months. While he was cautiously optimistic, he couldn't dismiss the possibility of lingering psychological distress or the supernatural forces that Amelia believed she was entangled with.

After a moment of contemplating silence.

"I will grant your request to be released, Amelia," Dr. Roberts finally said, his voice firm yet compassionate. "But it will be under the condition that you continue your therapy sessions on an outpatient basis. We will closely monitor your progress, and if there are any signs of distress or relapse, we will reevaluate your situation."

"Thank you, Dr. Roberts," Amelia replied, her voice filled with gratitude. "I am committed to my healing journey, and I will not take this opportunity for granted. I appreciate your belief in me."

Amelia stepped out of the psychiatric ward, her heart pounding with a mix of relief and trepidation. She had convinced Dr. Roberts that she was ready to be released, but the memory of the hooded figure and the haunting music box tune lingered in the depths of her mind. She knew that they were still a part of her reality, even if others couldn't see or hear them.

As Amelia stepped out of the hospital, Lily greeted her with a warm smile, her vibrant blue hair contrasting with her rebellious yet caring personality. "Hey, Mel! Ready to get out of this place and have some real fun?"

Lily, Amelia's childhood friend, had always been a free spirit, unafraid to tread the unconventional path. She had her share of struggles, but deep down, Amelia knew that Lily had a strong sense of loyalty and an innate ability to see beyond the surface.

Amelia's smile was tinged with hesitation, knowing that she was about to bring Lily into a world of danger and the supernatural. "Lily, there's something I need to tell you. It's about what happened in Spain."

Lily's eyes widened with curiosity. "I've always had a knack for finding trouble, and you've always stood by my side. So, I'm here for you, no matter what. Spill the beans."

Amelia smiled with relief. "Come on, the car is this way." Lily gestured with a wave of her arm. As Amelia followed, a sense of uncertainty came over her; she questioned Lily's willingness to understand, her willingness to believe, the tale that was about to unfold before her.

Amelia and Lily sat at a corner booth in a dimly lit bar, their drinks clinking as they toasted to their reunion. The atmosphere was lively, with the sound of music and laughter filling the air. For a moment, Amelia allowed herself to forget about the haunting experiences that had plagued her.

Lily, her long-time friend, had always been there for Amelia during their tumultuous teenage years. They had drifted apart in recent years, but now fate had brought them back together.

Amelia took a sip of her drink, her gaze fixed on Lily. "It's been so long, Lily. I've missed you. Thanks for being here for me."

Lily smirked mischievously, her eyes sparkling. "Ah, don't mention it, Mel. You know I can't resist a good adventure. So, spill the beans. What's been happening with you?"

Amelia hesitated, unsure of how to begin. She had always been the level-headed one, and recounting her encounters with the hooded figure seemed almost unbelievable. But she trusted Lily, and she needed someone who would listen without judgment.

Taking a deep breath, Amelia started, her words initially cautious yet earnest. "Lily, I've been going through some...strange and frightening things. I don't know how to explain it, but there's this hooded figure that's been haunting me. It's connected to a cursed music box, and I can hear its tune whenever something bad is about to happen." Amelia couldn't help but blurt the rest out.

Lily's eyebrows shot up, a mix of surprise and concern crossing her face. "Whoa, Mel, that's heavy stuff. Are you sure you're okay? You're not just pulling my leg, right?"

Amelia shook her head, her eyes filled with sincerity. "I wish I were joking, Lily. But it's real. I've been seeing things, hearing things. I even hurt someone, though I swear it wasn't intentional. The doctors, they think it's all in my head. But I know it's not. I need to find a way to break this curse."

Lily's expression softened, her playful demeanor giving way to empathy. She reached out and squeezed Amelia's hand. "Amelia, I may not understand all of this, but I trust you. I've seen you go through tough times before, and you've always come out stronger. We'll figure this out, together."

Amelia smiled, grateful for Lily's support. "Thank you, Lily. It means the world to me."

As the night wore on, Amelia and Lily shared stories, laughter, and even a few tears. They reminisced about their wild adventures from their youth, finding solace in the familiarity of their friendship.

Amelia knew that breaking the curse would not be easy. It would require facing her deepest fears, delving into the unknown, and perhaps even making sacrifices along the way. But with Lily by her side, Amelia felt a glimmer of hope.

Lily drove Amelia back home. The car ride was a peaceful quiet. As they pulled up, Amelia hesitated before stepping out. Amelia's heart fluttered with a mix of anticipation and anxiety as she walked through the front door of her home, Lily by her side. The familiar surroundings offered a sense of comfort.

As she entered the living room, Amelia noticed a letter on the coffee table. Her breath caught in her throat. It was from Carlos. With trembling hands, she picked it up and began to read, her eyes scanning the words that carried the weight of his emotions. Amelia's heart sank as she read Carlos's letter. She understood his need for space and reflection, but it was difficult to bear the thought of being separated from him during such a challenging time.

Lily noticed Amelia's distress and gently placed a comforting hand on her shoulder. "I'm sorry, Mel. I know how much you care about Carlos. But right now, let's focus on taking care of you. You don't have to be alone tonight. I'll stay with you."

Amelia's eyes welled up with gratitude as she looked at Lily, feeling an overwhelming sense of support. "Thank you, Lily. You being here means a lot to me. I don't know what I would do without you."

Lily smiled warmly. "That's what friends are for, right? To be there for each other no matter what. Let's put on a movie, order some takeout, and try to take our minds off things for a little while."

Amelia nodded, appreciating Lily's effort to bring some normalcy to their evening. They settled into the cozy living room, with the TV casting a soft glow as they chose a lighthearted comedy. As the laughter filled the room, Amelia's worries temporarily subsided. A recipe for a good night's rest.

Amelia's eyes shot open, her heart pounding in her chest as a peculiar sound echoed through the room. It was a low, scraping noise, like claws against a hard surface. She glanced over at Lily, still peacefully asleep, oblivious to the disturbance. "What time is it," Amelia muttered to herself, glancing at the clock placed atop the couch side table showing three a.m.

Slipping off of the couch, Amelia tiptoed toward the kitchen. Her throat dry and lips chapped, it was as if she had been lost in a desert; every ounce of water from her body had been drained away. She grabbed a cup from the cupboard and poured herself a cool glass of water, the condensation building up a droplet on the outside of the glass.

As she gulped down the water, a sense of relief washed over her; every cell in her body revitalized with every sip. She chuckled to herself trying to remember what woke her in the first place. She shrugged it off as her imagination and headed back to the living room.

Amelia froze in her tracks, the glass of water in her hand trembling. Her heart raced as the familiar tune of the music box pierced through the static on the television. A chill ran down her spine, and she could feel the weight of the curse resurfacing. Glancing at Lily, still peacefully asleep on the couch, panic and fear welled up within her, but she knew she couldn't let it consume her.

She rushed towards the television, desperately attempting to turn it off, but the remote seemed unresponsive. The haunting melody grew louder, filling the room with its eerie presence. The room seemed to grow colder as the music box tune permeated the airwaves, cutting through the static like a chilling reminder of the curse that continued to haunt her. Fear tightened its grip around her heart as she watched the television screen, the flickering images barely visible through the distortion.

Amelia's hands trembled as she unplugged the television, hoping to silence the song, but to no avail. The music continued, emanating from the now lifeless screen.

The room seemed to darken as shadows danced in the corners, taking on sinister forms that seemed to mock her. The melody, once enchanting, now held a malevolent power, its haunting notes resonating with a palpable sense of dread. Every fiber of Amelia's being screamed at her to run, to escape the clutches of this relentless curse, but she felt paralyzed, unable to tear her gaze away from the screen.

As the song continued to play, Amelia's mind raced, desperately seeking a way to break free from this nightmarish cycle. The once familiar and comforting space of her home now felt like a labyrinth of dangers, each step potentially leading her closer to her doom. Her heart pounded in her chest, the music box tune serving as a relentless reminder of the imminent threat that followed her every move.

Suddenly the room fell silent. Amelia felt for a brief moment that she had gone deaf, interrupted by a static buzz seemingly building up in her head. Amelia's blood ran cold as she turned her gaze towards the corner of the room, her heart pounding with a mix of terror and defiance. The sight of the hooded figure standing there, its sinister smile etched onto its concealed face, would make knees weak even of the most powerful men and women.

"What do you want from me?" Amelia managed to whisper, her voice laced with a combination of fear and anger. She knew that this encounter was not a mere coincidence. The hooded figure had returned to taunt her, to remind her of the inescapable grip of the curse that had plagued her existence.

The figure's eyes gleamed with an otherworldly light as it took a step closer, its voice a chilling whisper that seemed to echo within the depths of her mind. "Dance with me, Amelia. Embrace the inevitable. Your fate is sealed."

All Amelia could do was scream. Her scream pierced the air, carrying her terror and desperation. Her heart raced as she sprinted towards the front door, the instinct for self-preservation overriding all rational thought. But in her haste, her footing betrayed her, and she stumbled, her body crashing to the ground with a thud.

Pain seared through Amelia's body as she lay sprawled on the cold pavement, her palms scraped and bloodied from the fall. The impact jolted her back to reality, a harsh reminder of the dangers that lurked within and without. She fought against the rising panic, struggling to regain her composure and summon the strength to continue.

As Amelia slowly pushed herself up, her gaze turned to the open doorway behind her. The hooded figure, its twisted smile etched into her memory, stood ominously within the threshold. Its presence seemed to loom larger, the weight of its intentions suffocating the air.

As Amelia's trembling body propelled her forward, she abandoned any notion of graceful movement and resorted to crawling on her hands and knees. Her palms scraped against the rough pavement, leaving trails of blood behind, but the pain became inconsequential in the face of her overwhelming fear.

Every inch gained brought her closer to escape, her mind fixated on reaching safety. The rhythmic sound of her gasping breaths and the rapid beating of her heart filled her ears, drowning out the haunting melody that still lingered in the air. With each desperate crawl, she distanced herself from the hooded figure's menacing presence, only stopping and turning when she made it to the other side of the road. Amelia sat on the sidewalk opposite of her home, her face in her hands.

"AMELIA," the voice yelled from the porch; she was unwilling to open her eyes. "AMELIA, OPEN YOUR EYES," the voice yelled again.

"Please, just make it stop," a soft plea whimpered from Amelia's mouth. Desperation getting the better of her, Amelia outstretched her arms, embracing the fate to come.

"Mel, look at me."

Hesitant, Amelia opened her eyes. She could barely make out the figure standing on the porch, her eyes filled to the brim with tears. Amelia rubbed her eyes, and there standing where the hooded figure once stood was Lily.

A look of concern and helplessness draped over Lily's face. Amelia just cried, unable to say what had happened. All she could utter was a "He's here," each word interrupted by a loud sniffle.

"Mel, the hooded figure is not real," Lily said scoldingly. "It's all in your head. It can't hurt you," Lily said reassuringly.

Just then a deep gurgle echoed throughout the depths of the house, sending a sense of impending doom throughout Lily's body. "Oh, I'm real, as real as the air that you breathe or the leaves on the tree. I'm the beginning and the end. I am your death," a disembodied voice said, chuckling menacingly afterwards.

Lily turned to face the empty doorway. The color of her face seemed to run away in fear. Lily desperately tried to see where the voice was coming from. The rooms seemed void of any light. An inky blackness took the place of any recognizable walls or furniture.

"Mmm, and by the look on your face I'm real enough for you too," the voice said mockingly.

Thumps began to echo. Something was coming towards the doorway.

With every audible step forward, Lily followed with a step back, all the while whispering, "This isn't real," while intensely watching the door.

A chilling breeze swept through the air, sending shivers down her spine, momentarily breaking her gaze of the door. In that instant, the figure appeared. Standing there, its form draped in darkness. Lily summoned her courage and stepped forward.

Lily was always the brave one, always willing to take the fall, take the hit for Amelia, and this time was no different. "I don't know who you are, but you will leave my friend alone," Lily said confidently.

With a determined stride, Lily approached the figure, her eyes locked onto its concealed face. "Lily!" Amelia shouted, a desperate plea for her to stop, to turn and run as far away as she could.

Lily turned to Amelia. "Everything is going to be okay, Mel."

In that moment Amelia believed her, and a glimmer of hope sparked in her heart.

Lily reached out, her trembling hand inching closer to the hood that obscured its true visage. As her fingers grazed the fabric, she firmly gripped it, ready to reveal the grotesque truth hidden within.

With a swift motion, Lily pulled back the hood, exposing the figure's face to the dim light. What she beheld was a horrifying sight that sent a surge of revulsion coursing through her veins. The face before her was disfigured and twisted, its features contorted into a nightmarish mask of decay and malice. Lily could see the grotesque mess that lay beneath, a sight that only she could witness.

As Lily stared, her mind racing to understand what was standing before her, the face smiled. A gasp escaped Lily's lips as she recoiled, her heart pounding in her chest. The sight before her was a manifestation of the darkness that had haunted Amelia, a physical representation of the curse that had tormented her. The bravery Lily held a moment ago now vanished. The strength in her legs crumbled as she stumbled back, unable to regain her balance. "LILY!" Amelia helplessly screamed, watching her best friend, her sister, stumble into the street.

SCREEEEEECH.

Chapter Five

CONFRONTING THE PAST

Amelia's heart sank as she sat in the back of the ambulance, a numbness enveloping her as she stared blankly at the tragic scene unfolding before her. The flashing lights and blaring sirens created a surreal backdrop to the lifeless form of her dear friend, Lily, sprawled on the unforgiving asphalt. Bloodied and battered, with her limbs bent in inhuman ways. The bus that had struck her came to a halt a few feet ahead, its presence a haunting reminder of the fragility of life. Amelia's heart shattered as she realized that the hooded figure's reach had claimed yet another victim, leaving her alone once again in the relentless grip of darkness.

"Hello, I'm detective Hunter Blackwood. Can you tell me what happened?" Amelia looked up. She immediately noticed his scars contrasting with his smooth complexion, matching the raspy voice she heard. His eyes, deep and sincere, were filled with the harsh experiences of his job. She felt safe. She didn't know why, but she felt like she could trust him. She desperately wanted to tell him the truth but knew she couldn't.

Amelia, her voice trembling with a mix of fear and desperation, concocted a story for the detective, desperately avoiding the truth that lurked in the shadows. With tear-filled eyes, she explained that Lily had mistakenly walked into the street, her mind preoccupied, in an attempt to reach her parked car. She painted a picture of a tragic accident born out of her own distraction, hoping to shield the detective from the sinister reality that had claimed Lily's life. Deep down, Amelia knew the truth would only bring more danger, and for now, she had to protect herself and anyone who dared to stand by her side.

Detective Blackwood, with his sharp intuition and keen investigative instincts, couldn't shake the feeling that Amelia's account was incomplete. His gaze pierced through her tear-stained eyes, searching for any hint of deception. He knew there was more to the story than what she was revealing, but he also sensed her deep-seated fear and the need to shield herself from a hidden truth. With a reluctant nod, he decided to tread cautiously.

"Okay, I'll reach back out if anything comes up," he said.

Amelia watched as detective Blackwood walked back to his car, her sense of safety going with him. A part of her desperately wanted to shout for him to stop, to tell him of the hooded figure, of the curse, that her friend didn't die from an accident but was murdered. She understood that in doing so would put his life in danger; Lily's death made that evident enough.

Amelia checked into a hotel room, unable to return home, the weight of her sorrow and the burden of the curse heavy upon her shoulders. As she sat on the edge of the bed, her mind racing with thoughts and memories, she realized that she couldn't escape the clutches of the curse without confronting its origins. The haunting tune, the hooded figure, and the relentless traps of fate all traced back to that Spanish market. Determination ignited within her. She knew she had to return to that place, to delve into its secrets and unearth the key to breaking the curse.

With a heavy heart, Amelia made the difficult decision to embark on this perilous journey alone. She knew that involving others would only put them in harm's way. Armed with her resolve and a newfound determination, she made plans to return to Spain, the land where her fate had taken a treacherous turn. It was a daunting task, but Amelia was ready to face the unknown, to navigate the intricate web of death traps that awaited her, and to unlock the secrets that lay dormant in the heart of that Spanish market.

Leaving behind her life, her loved ones, and the safety of familiarity, Amelia set forth on her solitary quest. Though fear threatened to consume her, she drew strength from the flickering flame of hope that burned within. She knew the road ahead would be fraught with danger, both physical and metaphysical, but she was determined to face it head-on. In her heart, she held onto the belief that within the depths of the market's enigmatic knick-knacks and the haunting melody of the music box, lay the answers she sought—the key to breaking the curse and freeing herself from the suffocating grip of destiny.

As the plane soared through the skies, carrying Amelia back to Spain, a mixture of anticipation and trepidation filled her heart. She gazed out of the window, the sprawling landscape below serving as a reminder of the daunting path she had chosen. The memories of that fateful day in the Spanish market flooded her mind, but this time, she was armed with determination and a newfound purpose. She vowed to not only break the curse that plagued her, but to ensure that no one else would suffer its malevolent grasp.

Stepping onto Spanish soil once again, Amelia took a deep breath, grounding herself in the familiar, yet haunting atmosphere. With each step, she felt the weight of her past and the weight of her mission intertwine. She knew that the road ahead would be filled with perilous challenges, each one intricately woven into the fabric of fate. But she refused to be deterred. She sought redemption not just for herself, but for Lily as well, whose life was cut so short in the crossfire.

Guided by her instincts and a growing sense of purpose, Amelia delved deep into the maze-like streets of the Spanish market. She retraced her steps, searching for the elusive figure disguised as an old man, the purveyor of the cursed music box. Determined to unravel the mysteries and break the cycle of death, she braced herself for the trials that awaited her. Armed with a heart full of resilience and a spirit fueled by the desire to protect others, Amelia embarked on a journey that would test her to her very core, in her quest to triumph over the curse and forge a path towards a brighter, safer future._

Chapter Six

SECRETS OF RINCÓN
DEL OLVIDO

As Amelia ventured into the town of Rincón del Olvido, she found it shrouded in an eerie silence. The narrow streets were lined with quaint houses, and the locals seemed to carry a sense of secrecy in their eyes. Determined to uncover any legends or tales related to the music box and the hooded figure, she approached the townspeople with cautious curiosity.

Amelia's inquiries led her to an elderly woman named Isabella, who was known for her knowledge of local folklore. Isabella welcomed Amelia into her home cluttered with ancient books and artifacts. As they sat surrounded by the musty scent of old parchment, Isabella began recounting a tale passed down through generations.

According to legend, the music box was said to hold a cursed melody, capable of ensnaring souls and bringing forth the presence of Death itself. The hooded figure, known as the Reaper's Messenger, was said to be an agent of fate, tasked with marking those destined to die. However, the Reaper's Messenger grew greedy; it began to enjoy the suffering of humans, watching them fight to survive, feeding an insatiable hunger for pain and fear.

When Death discovered what the Messenger had done, it was outraged. The Messenger had tainted Death's name, the art of life passing itself. Death attempted to banish the Messenger to an endless void, but before doing so the Messenger sealed a part of itself in the music box. Now the Messenger, growing stronger with every victim that falls to the curse of the music box, hopes to one day break free from the music box so that it may once again wreak havoc and feed on the suffering of mortals.

Amelia listened intently, her heart pounding with a mixture of fear and determination. Isabella suggested that the answers Amelia sought might lie within the town's old library, which held forgotten volumes and secrets waiting to be discovered.

Inspired by Isabella's words, Amelia made her way to the ancient library. Dusty shelves lined with forgotten tomes filled the room, and the scent of aged paper filled the air. She spent hours poring over fragile manuscripts, searching for any mention of the music box or the hooded figure. With each turn of the page, the secrets of Rincón del Olvido slowly unraveled before her eyes, leading her closer to the truth she so desperately sought.

Amelia, happy with the progress she'd made for the day, headed back to the hotel. She didn't realize that the sun had already begun to set, lost in the pages and notes of the old library. As she stepped out of the building, a mysterious figure jumped from the shadows and grabbed her from behind.

Amelia's heart raced as the mysterious figure's grip tightened around her. Panic surged through her veins, but a voice in the back of her mind urged her to stay calm and assess the situation. With a deep breath, she steadied herself and carefully observed her surroundings, searching for any signs of danger.

The figure, cloaked in darkness, whispered urgent words into Amelia's ear, warning her of the dangers that awaited her. Fear mingled with curiosity as she hesitated for a moment, contemplating her next move. In the end, her determination to uncover the truth propelled her forward, overriding the fear that threatened to paralyze her.

Trusting her instincts, Amelia made the decision to follow the mysterious figure. They moved swiftly through the dimly lit streets, their footsteps echoing in the stillness of the night. Shadows danced on the walls, concealing their path from prying eyes. Amelia couldn't help but wonder who this enigmatic stranger was and what their true intentions might be.

As they ventured deeper into the labyrinthine alleys, Amelia's mind raced with questions. Who was this figure, and why had they chosen to intervene at this crucial moment? What secrets had she uncovered that made her a target? Yet, the urgency in the figure's voice convinced her that their guidance was her best chance at survival.

Finally, they arrived at an old church, its stone walls worn by time. The figure pushed open a hidden door, revealing a hidden passage that descended into darkness. Amelia's heart raced as they entered the secret chamber together, the scent of damp stone and old wood filling the air.

As the mysterious figure led Amelia through the hidden passageways beneath the old church, they finally arrived in a secret chamber bathed in moonlight. The atmosphere crackled with anticipation as Amelia's eyes adjusted to the dimly lit surroundings. The figure turned to face her, stepping into the moonbeam's embrace, revealing their true identity.

"My name is Emilio, but my friends call me Milo," the figure spoke softly, his voice carrying a sense of both wisdom and sorrow. He had not only survived the curse but had also found a way to defy its grip. Amelia's heart swelled with a mixture of relief and hope, grateful for the unexpected ally she had found on her perilous journey.

Milo explained that he, too, had been marked by the curse, haunted by the same music box tune and pursued by the hooded figure. However, through years of relentless pursuit for answers, he had uncovered the secrets needed to survive the curse. His determination and resilience had led him to this pivotal moment, where he could now guide Amelia towards her own salvation.

Milo explained the church offered a momentary respite from the relentless pursuit of the curse, a sanctuary where the Messenger's reach was momentarily severed. Milo, understanding the gravity of the situation, extended an invitation for Amelia to stay and find solace within the ancient walls. But Amelia's resolve burned fiercely within her. She knew that simply hiding away would not bring an end to the curse that had haunted her existence.

Declining Milo's offer, Amelia explained that her purpose was not to seek safety or temporary refuge. She yearned for a permanent solution, a way to break the curse's grip on not just herself, but on anyone else who might fall victim to its malevolence. She could not bear the thought of another innocent soul enduring the torment she had faced.

As Amelia shared her unwavering determination to break the curse, Milo's frustration began to surface, causing a shadow to fall over his countenance. He sighed heavily, the weight of his own past experiences evident in his voice. Milo confessed that despite his years of relentless pursuit, they had come to a painful realization—there was no true victory, only temporary reprieve.

With a heavy heart, Milo recounted the losses he had endured in his quest to overcome the curse. Friends, loved ones, and countless others had fallen victim to the relentless grasp of fate. Each attempt to break free had ended in failure, leaving Milo haunted by the weight of his inability to protect those he cared for.

Milo's frustration was rooted in the bitter truth he had come to accept—the curse was a formidable force that defied conventional means of defeat. Its power was far-reaching, entangled with the fabric of destiny itself. While temporary measures could be taken to stall its progress, true liberation remained an elusive dream.

As Amelia absorbed Milo's words, a wave of desolation washed over her. Doubt began to gnaw at the edges of her resolve. She had been fueled by the hope of a permanent solution, but now faced the daunting reality that perhaps there was no ultimate victory to be attained.

Yet, within that moment of despair, Amelia's determination rekindled like a flickering flame. She refused to accept defeat without exhausting every possibility. While she understood the futility of a straightforward triumph over the curse, she believed that there must be a way to mitigate its impact, to protect those she cared for, and to break free from its suffocating grasp, even if only for a fleeting moment. With a newfound resolve, Amelia vowed to forge her own path, driven by the belief that even in the face of insurmountable odds, there was a glimmer of hope waiting to be discovered.

Amelia's perseverance inspired Milo. Her will instilled a hope inside his heart that Milo thought was long gone. "Okay, I will help," said Milo. Embracing the newfound strength brought on by Amelia's confidence.

"If we work together, I just know we'll figure out the next piece of the puzzle," Amelia said confidently.

Amelia and Milo immersed themselves in the task at hand, their collective determination shining brightly. Hours turned into a blur as they meticulously studied the fragments of information they had gathered, connecting the dots like an intricate puzzle. Each clue, each symbol, held a piece of the truth they sought.

In a moment of profound clarity, the realization struck them like lightning. The key to banishing the Messenger lay hidden within the knowledge of its true name. It was a name that held power, a name that Death itself had failed to utter. With this newfound understanding, Amelia and Milo embarked on a quest to uncover the name that would dismantle the curse's grip once and for all._

Chapter Seven
A NAME UNUTTERED

With newfound determination burning in their hearts, Amelia proposed seeking the guidance of Isabella, the wise old lady revered for her knowledge of ancient folklore and mystical realms. Milo readily agreed, recognizing the depth of Isabella's wisdom and the potential insights she could offer. Together, they set out on a quest to find the elusive Isabella, hoping that she held the missing piece of the puzzle they sought.

Their journey took them through winding paths, as if the very nature around them acknowledged the importance of their mission. Finally, they arrived at Isabella's secluded cottage, nestled amidst ancient trees and whispered legends. With bated breath, they approached the door, anticipation mingling with a glimmer of hope.

Amelia's heart skipped a beat as she noticed the slightly ajar door to Isabella's home. A feeling of unease settled in the pit of her stomach. With caution in their steps, she and Milo approached the entrance, their senses on high alert. It was unlike Isabella to leave her door open, and they couldn't ignore the nagging suspicion that something was amiss.

Amelia's heart sank as she and Milo pushed open the creaking door to Isabella's home. The scene that unfolded before them was a harrowing sight—a once tranquil abode now in disarray, its serenity shattered. The air was heavy with an ominous presence that sent shivers down their spines.

Their eyes met with the lifeless gaze of Isabella, her face frozen in a state of eternal terror. The brutality of the scene made it clear that she had met a gruesome fate. The room itself bore the marks of a violent struggle, furniture overturned and cherished possessions scattered haphazardly. It was a chilling testament to the malevolence that lurked in the shadows.

Grief and anger swelled within Amelia as she knelt beside Isabella's lifeless body, her hands trembling. Isabella had been a source of wisdom, a beacon of hope in their quest. Now, her knowledge and guidance were lost forever, stolen by the merciless hands of the unknown assailant.

As Amelia and Milo stood in the shattered remnants of Isabella's home, a heavy silence settled between them. Amelia had no idea of the deep connection that bound Milo to Isabella, and the weight of the revelation now hung in the air. Milo's gaze met Amelia's, his eyes revealing a mixture of grief and determination.

Slowly, Milo began to unravel the well-guarded secret that he had kept hidden from Amelia all this time. Isabella was not just a wise old lady to him; she was his beloved grandmother, a guiding force in his life. Milo had kept their familial bond a secret to protect Isabella from the dangers that lurked within their shared pursuit. He had tried to shield her from the darkness that had consumed so many others.

The revelation shook Amelia to her core, realizing the profound sacrifice that Milo had made in the name of their shared mission. Isabella had not only been Amelia's beacon of wisdom but also a beloved figure in Milo's life, a source of unconditional love and support. The weight of their shared loss deepened their resolve to uncover the truth and seek justice for Isabella's tragic end.

Grief mingled with determination as they vowed to continue Isabella's and Lily's legacies, to honor their memories, and to put an end to the Messenger's reign of terror. The bond between Amelia and Milo grew stronger, forged by their shared loss and the desire to protect those they held dear. In their hearts, they carried the spirits of Isabella and Lily, a legacy of strength and resilience that would guide them through the darkest of times.

Amelia's hands trembled as she sifted through the wreckage of Isabella's home, her eyes scanning every corner for a clue that would lead them closer to the Messenger's true name. The shattered artifacts and scattered books seemed to hold fragments of Isabella's wisdom, waiting to be discovered. Determined, Amelia pushed aside her grief and focused on the task at hand.

With each item she examined, memories of her conversations with Isabella flooded back, their discussions about the ancient texts and folklore that might hold the key to unraveling the Messenger's mystery. Amelia's mind raced, connecting the dots between the fragments of knowledge she had gathered over the course of their journey. She knew that hidden within Isabella's belongings lay the answer they sought.

As she rummaged through a pile of charred books, Amelia's eyes caught sight of a handwritten journal partially burned but still intact. With bated breath, she delicately opened the pages, revealing Isabella's meticulous notes and findings. The journal held a wealth of information, cryptic symbols, and references to ancient rituals. This was the key they had been searching for.

Amelia and Milo huddled together, pouring over the journal's pages, piecing together the fragments of Isabella's research. The clues slowly revealed a pattern, leading them to a forgotten monastery deep in the heart of the Spanish countryside. It was there, amidst the sacred walls, that the Messenger's true name was said to be hidden. Amelia's heart raced with anticipation as she realized they were on the brink of a breakthrough.

Armed with Isabella's journal and a newfound determination, Amelia and Milo set out towards the monastery, their spirits lifted by the prospect of unveiling the Messenger's true name. The path ahead was treacherous, but their unwavering resolve pushed them forward. They were prepared to face any challenge, to navigate the labyrinthine corridors of the ancient monastery, and to uncover the secret that would bring an end to the Messenger.

As the night settled around them, Amelia and Milo sat by the crackling campfire, their faces illuminated by the dancing flames. The air was filled with a sense of camaraderie as they shared stories of their lives before the curse had turned their worlds upside down. In the flickering firelight, their bond deepened, and a glimmer of hope shone through the darkness that had consumed their journey thus far.

Amelia spoke of her childhood dreams, her aspirations, and the moments of joy that had shaped her life. With a wistful smile, she recounted the adventures she had imagined and the endless possibilities that once seemed within her grasp. Milo listened attentively, captivated by the strength and resilience that Amelia had demonstrated throughout their tumultuous journey together.

In turn, Milo opened up about his own past, sharing memories of his grandmother Isabella and the wisdom she had imparted upon him. He spoke of a time when the curse was unknown to them, and life held a sense of normalcy. Their laughter mingled with the crackling fire, creating a refuge from the shadows that threatened to engulf them.

As the night wore on, their stories became a tapestry of shared experiences and unspoken understanding. They found solace in each other's presence, a fleeting respite from the trials that lay ahead. In those moments, it felt as if time stood still, and the weight of their burdens was momentarily lifted. Their connection deepened, reminding them of the strength that could be found in companionship.

Underneath the starlit sky, Amelia and Milo forged a bond that transcended the curse that had brought them together. In the midst of their shared stories and the flickering flames, they discovered a glimmer of hope, a reminder that even in the face of darkness, human connection could provide a beacon of light. With renewed determination, they made a silent vow to protect each other, drawing strength from the newfound bond they had formed.

Their shared laughter was like a sweet lullaby, inevitably putting both of them in a well-deserved sleep.

Startled from his slumber, Milo's eyes darted around the darkness, searching for the source of the eerie voice that had penetrated his dreams. The voice echoed in his mind, its haunting melody filled with both familiarity and an unsettling unknown. With a racing heart, he listened intently, his senses on high alert.

As the whispers of the woman's voice grew louder, Milo felt a strange mix of apprehension and curiosity. He slowly rose from his sleeping bag, his steps cautious as he followed the ethereal sound. It seemed to lead him further away from the campsite, deeper into the surrounding woods where the moonlight struggled to penetrate the dense canopy above.

Branches rustled and leaves crunched underfoot as Milo navigated the unfamiliar terrain, his senses keenly attuned to the voice that beckoned him onward. Each step brought him closer to the enigmatic presence, his mind racing with questions and a tingling anticipation. There was an undeniable connection between the voice and his own family history, a sensation that tugged at his very core.

As he neared a clearing bathed in a soft, silvery glow. There, standing amidst the moonlit mist, was a spectral figure.

Chapter Eight
AN INTANGIBLE SACRIFICE

Her features were hazy, her form translucent, yet her presence held a certain gravitas. The woman's voice resonated with a bittersweet melody, wrapping itself around Milo's being, whispering secrets from a time long forgotten.

Torn between trepidation and an inexplicable yearning, Milo stepped forward, his voice trembling as he spoke. "Who are you? Why have you called out to me?" he questioned, his words barely a whisper. The woman's ethereal figure swayed gently, as if in response, her eyes filled with a mixture of sorrow and purpose.

Milo's eyes widened as the spectral figure transformed into the familiar countenance of Isabella, his late grandmother. Her translucent form flickered with a mix of concern and urgency, her eyes conveying a warning. Isabella's voice, though ethereal, carried a sense of urgency as she spoke.

"The Messenger knows," Isabella whispered, her voice carrying a weight of foreboding. "It senses your intentions and seeks to thwart you. You must act swiftly if you are to succeed in your quest."

Milo's mind raced as he processed the gravity of his grandmother's words. The realization that their plans had been compromised filled him with a mixture of determination and unease. The Messenger's relentless pursuit had now taken a more sinister turn, as it actively sought to disrupt their mission to uncover its true name and banish it for eternity.

Gathering his wits, Milo locked eyes with Isabella's translucent form, his voice filled with a resolute determination. "We cannot falter now. We have come too far to turn back. The Messenger will not deter us from our purpose. We will press on."

Isabella's spectral form nodded in agreement, her eyes filled with a mix of pride and concern. She reached out a spectral hand, placing it gently on Milo's shoulder, a comforting touch that belied the dire circumstances. "You carry our family's legacy, Milo. You possess the strength and resilience needed to face this challenge. Trust in your instincts and the knowledge we have passed down through generations."

As Milo bid a final farewell to his beloved grandmother, tears running down his cheeks, a sinister voice called out to them. "How sweet," it said.

Milo's heart skipped a beat as the sinister voice echoed through the night air. He turned swiftly, his eyes scanning the surroundings for the source of the chilling words. The voice dripped with malevolence, sending a shiver down his spine, and he felt a knot of unease tightening in the pit of his stomach.

In the shadows, a figure emerged, its presence oozing darkness and malice. It stepped forward, revealing itself to be the Messenger, cloaked in a tattered robe that billowed in an unseen wind. Its face concealed beneath a hood, leaving only a pair of piercing eyes that seemed to glow with an otherworldly light.

Milo clenched his fists, his resolve steeling against the Messenger's intimidating presence. "You will not intimidate me," he declared, his voice laced with determination. "We are prepared to face you and put an end to your reign."

The Messenger let out a chilling laugh that reverberated through the night. "Oh, how brave you are, little mortal," it sneered, its voice filled with disdain. "But your defiance means nothing. I have witnessed countless like you, foolishly believing they could defy the inevitable."

Milo's eyes narrowed as he met the Messenger's gaze, his voice unwavering. "We know something you fear, don't we? The knowledge of your true name being the key to your banishment. That's why you seek to silence us."

The Messenger's lips curled into a wicked smile, its eyes glinting with a mixture of malevolence and amusement. "Ah, the name. Do you truly believe it holds power over me? I have transcended names and become something far beyond your comprehension. Your feeble attempts to banish me will only bring you closer to your doom."

The Messenger lunged at Milo, its hand forming into a monstrous claw, ready to strike him down where he stood. However, to the Messenger's surprise, he could not touch him, an invisible force preventing it from moving any closer.

Isabella's spectral form stood tall and defiant, her presence radiating with a protective energy that seemed to shimmer in the air. Her voice echoed with a commanding authority as she stared down the Messenger, her eyes ablaze with a fierce will.

"You shall not harm my grandson, Messenger," Isabella's voice rang out, filled with a potent mix of love and defiance. "For years, my family has suffered under your curse, but no more. We will not yield to your malevolence."

The Messenger's eyes narrowed, its form shifting uneasily. "You dare to defy me, old spirit?" it hissed, its voice tinged with a mix of anger and disgust. "You are but a specter, a remnant of the past. Your power cannot match mine."

Isabella's ethereal figure glowed brighter, a subtle aura of ancient energy emanating from her. "The power of love and familial bonds transcends realms, Messenger," she declared, her voice filled with an unwavering conviction. "I am here to protect my grandson and aid him in his quest to rid the world of your curse."

With a sudden surge of energy, Isabella extended her spectral hand, sending a wave of energy rippling toward the Messenger. The dark entity recoiled, its form trembling as it struggled against the force of Isabella's will.

"You underestimate the strength of our love and determination," Milo interjected, his voice steady as he stood beside his spectral grandmother.

The Messenger let out a snarl, its form flickering with uncertainty. It realized that it was facing a formidable force, one fueled by love, resilience, and generations of pain. It took a step back, its confidence waning in the face of such unwavering determination.

With a lingering hiss, the Messenger receded into the shadows, its form dissipating into the darkness. But before completely fading away, it uttered a chilling warning that hung in the air like an ominous cloud.

"Relish in this moment, for I shall return," the Messenger's voice echoed, a haunting whisper. Milo yelled with joy, taking in the victory even if it was only momentarily. Milo turned to his grandmother hoping to celebrate with her.

His heart sank as he witnessed Isabella's spectral form fading before his eyes. The once vibrant presence that had protected him throughout this battle was now growing weaker, its essence dissipating into the air.

"Grandma..." Milo's voice trembled with a mixture of gratitude and sadness. "Thank you for everything you've done, for being there for me all these years."

Isabella's fading form offered a gentle smile, her voice filled with a bittersweet tenderness. "You have always carried my love and strength within you, my dear grandson," she whispered, her voice ethereal and distant. "It is time for me to rest, but remember that I am always with you in spirit."

Tears welled up in Milo's eyes as he reached out a hand toward the dissipating figure of his grandmother. He could feel the warmth of her love, the weight of her sacrifices, and the immeasurable bond they shared. He knew that he would miss her presence, but her spirit would forever reside within his heart.

As Isabella's form faded completely, Milo closed his eyes, cherishing the memories and the wisdom she had imparted upon him. He knew that her guidance would continue to guide him through the challenges ahead, even if he couldn't see her physically.

The last remnants of Isabella vanished; the sunrise began to peak over the mountains. The golden rays of the rising sun painted the sky in hues of pink and orange, casting a warm glow over the landscape. Signifying the hope that comes with a new day, laced with the bittersweet tears of a loved life lost.

Milo's footsteps were heavy as he made his way back to the camp, his mind swirling with conflicting emotions. He knew he had to tell Amelia about his encounter with the Messenger and the spectral presence of Isabella. Yet, a nagging doubt crept into his thoughts, causing him to hesitate.

As he approached, he saw her stomping out the remainder of the fire. Amelia turned to him with a smile, her eyes filled with warmth and trust. Milo's heart tightened at the sight of her, a pang of guilt tugging at his conscience. How could he keep such a significant experience hidden from her? But he couldn't bear the thought of burdening her with the weight of his encounter, knowing the toll it would take on her already weary spirit.

With each closing step, the secret weighed heavily on Milo's shoulders. He feared the repercussions of his silence, aware that honesty and open communication were essential for their journey together. Yet, he couldn't shake the fear of causing Amelia further distress or robbing her of the hope they both desperately clung to.

Amelia's eyes sparkled with anticipation as she looked at Milo. Her excitement tugged at his heart, reminding him of the purpose they shared. As she asked about his brief absence, a mixture of relief and apprehension washed over him. He took a moment to compose himself before answering.

"I went for a walk," Milo replied, his voice steady but his mind racing with thoughts. "I needed some time to clear my head, to gather my thoughts for the journey ahead. There's so much at stake, and I wanted to make sure I was prepared."

Amelia nodded, her eyes shining with enthusiasm. She sensed his underlying seriousness, but she chose to focus on the determination in his voice. "I understand," she said, her voice filled with unwavering support. "We have come so far, and we can't let anything distract us from our mission. Let's continue to the monastery and find the answers we seek."

Milo's heart swelled with gratitude for Amelia's understanding and unwavering commitment. He marveled at her strength and resolve, finding solace in her presence. The weight of his secret still lingered, but he found comfort in the knowledge that their shared purpose would guide them through the challenges ahead.

As they packed their belongings and prepared to resume their journey, Milo made a silent vow to himself. He would find the right moment to tell Amelia the truth, to lay bare the events he had witnessed. He knew that their bond could withstand the burden of his confession, and together, they would face whatever darkness awaited them._

Chapter Nine

TRIALS OF THE MONASTERY

Amelia and Milo stood before the grand entrance of the ancient monastery, their eyes wide with awe and reverence. The weathered stone walls and towering spires exuded an aura of mystique and wisdom. The air around them felt heavy with history and the weight of centuries-old secrets. As they crossed the threshold, the silence enveloped them, punctuated only by the soft echo of their footsteps on the worn floor.

Inside, the monastery revealed its intricate beauty, adorned with delicate tapestries, flickering candlelight, and the scent of aged books. Amelia's eyes were drawn to the ornate stained-glass windows that bathed the hallways in a kaleidoscope of colors, while Milo's gaze lingered on the ancient manuscripts displayed in glass cases. They felt as if they had stepped into a different realm, one where time stood still, and mysteries whispered in the shadows.

As Amelia and Milo explored the labyrinthine corridors of the monastery, they were met with a sense of overwhelming vastness. Countless rooms and chambers awaited their investigation, each holding the potential for hidden knowledge. They found themselves standing in a vast library, rows upon rows of shelves stacked high with ancient texts. The dusty air whispered stories of forgotten lore, and the dim lighting cast elongated shadows that seemed to dance among the bookcases. Unsure of where to begin, they started methodically scanning the titles, hoping to find a clue that would guide them on their quest.

They wandered from room to room, their fingers delicately tracing the spines of weathered books, hoping to stumble upon a forgotten manuscript that held the key to their quest. The musty scent of old parchment filled the air as they perused rows upon rows of ancient tomes, their eyes scanning pages filled with arcane symbols and cryptic illustrations. It was like searching for a needle in a haystack, their determination guiding them through the maze of forgotten knowledge. Yet, in the midst of their search, doubts crept into their minds, questioning if they would ever find the answers they sought within these abandoned halls.

As the sun began its descent, casting long shadows through the monastery's stained-glass windows, Amelia and Milo found themselves slumped against a weathered stone wall. The weight of their fruitless search hung heavy upon them, their exhaustion mirroring the fading light. They had combed through every nook and cranny, yet the elusive secrets of the Messenger remained stubbornly hidden.

Feeling defeated, they reluctantly accepted the reality that they would have to spend the night within the monastery's ancient walls. Settling down in a small chamber, they laid out their meager belongings and prepared to rest. Weariness washed over them, mingled with a tinge of disappointment, as they realized that their journey had hit a temporary impasse. Yet, in the midst of their dejected state, a glimmer of hope remained. They knew that the answer they sought might be just within their reach, waiting to be discovered in the light of a new day. With that flicker of optimism in their hearts, they closed their eyes, hoping that sleep would bring them the clarity they sought.

Amelia's eyes fluttered open, her senses alert as she strained to identify the source of the faint whispering that filled the air. Milo stirred beside her, also roused from his slumber by the mysterious voice. As they listened intently, the words grew clearer, beckoning them with an urgent call. Intrigued and hesitant, they followed the sound, their footsteps quiet and cautious.

Their search led them to a section of the monastery's wall that seemed ordinary, blending seamlessly with the rest of the structure. But as Amelia pressed her hand against the stone, she felt a subtle vibration, revealing a hidden mechanism. With a gentle push, the wall shifted, revealing a narrow passageway hidden in the shadows. Excitement mingled with uneasiness as they exchanged glances, their curiosity overpowering any fear they might have felt.

In silent agreement, they descended the staircase, their anticipation building with each step. The air grew heavy with a sense of foreboding, yet their resolve remained unshaken. The winding path led them through dimly lit corridors, their footsteps echoing in the quiet solitude. They couldn't help but wonder what lay ahead, what secrets this hidden sanctuary held, and whether it would finally unveil the true nature of their elusive adversary.

Amelia and Milo continued their descent through the winding staircase, their steps seemingly endless. The passage seemed to stretch on for hours, time becoming an elusive concept as they delved deeper into the depths of the monastery. Their hearts pounded in their chests, a mix of excitement and trepidation intertwining within them.

As they rounded another bend, the corridor abruptly opened up, revealing a breathtaking sight. Before them lay a vast underground cavern, its expanse stretching far beyond the reach of the feeble torchlight for the wall. Stalactites hung from the ceiling like ancient sentinels, casting eerie shadows across the rugged terrain. The air was cool and damp, carrying whispers of forgotten tales and hidden truths.

Amelia and Milo stood at the precipice of this enigmatic underworld, captivated by the grandeur before them. They couldn't help but feel a sense of awe and insignificance in the face of such vastness. The cavern seemed to hold the weight of ages, concealing secrets that had long been guarded by time itself. It was in this moment that they knew they were on the brink of a profound discovery—one that would either grant them the knowledge to vanquish the Messenger or plunge them deeper into its clutches.

Amelia and Milo cautiously ventured further into the cavern, their eyes fixated on the intricate structures that adorned the walls. The carvings seemed to tell a story—a narrative etched into the very stone. Symbolic images depicted figures in various poses, scenes of struggle and triumph, and a recurring motif of a hooded figure looming over them all. The craftsmanship was remarkable, a testament to the skill and dedication of those who had created it.

As they followed the path outlined by the carvings, the atmosphere grew heavier, the air charged with a sense of ancient power. The cavern seemed to pulsate with a mysterious energy, as if it held the echoes of forgotten rituals and long-lost wisdom. Amelia and Milo's steps were cautious yet determined, their anticipation building with each passing moment.

The cavern continued to unveil its secrets as they moved deeper into its depths. They encountered chambers filled with cryptic symbols and inscriptions, enigmatic diagrams that hinted at hidden knowledge. The walls seemed to whisper secrets of old, their voices barely audible yet resonating within the very core of Amelia and Milo's beings. It was as if the cavern itself was guiding them, leading them closer to the truth they sought.

They continued along the path before them, taking in the scene as they carried on. The path eventually led them to a structure carved into the walls of the cavern. Amelia's and Milo's eyes widened as they entered the chamber and beheld the sight before them.

Amelia and Milo approached the room cautiously, their eyes fixed on the mysterious black book that sat on the pedestal in the center. The book seemed to emanate an otherworldly aura. Milo reached out and carefully lifted the book, feeling a surge of anticipation course through him. A chill ran through his fingertips, sending a shiver down his spine. The room seemed to hold its breath, as if aware of the significance of this moment.

As soon as Milo touched the book, a series of tremors rattled the cavern, causing the ground to shake violently. The walls began to crumble, sending cascades of rocks and dust into the air. Amelia and Milo exchanged alarmed glances, realizing that their search had triggered a cataclysmic event. Time seemed to slow as they rushed to find an escape route, desperately navigating through the collapsing passages.

The deafening sound of crumbling stone and the dust-filled air engulfed them as they raced against the impending collapse of the cavern. The weight of their discovery hung heavy in their hearts as they fought their way through the chaos. Every step felt like an eternity, the fear of being trapped beneath tons of rock threatening to overtake them. They pushed forward, driven by sheer determination and the hope of survival.

Amelia and Milo scrambled up the secret staircase, their hearts pounding in their chests. They could feel the reverberations of the collapsing cavern behind them, urging them to move faster. With each step, the ancient stone stairs creaked beneath their weight, as if protesting their frantic ascent.

As they burst back into the main chambers of the monastery, they were greeted with a scene of chaos. The once-sturdy walls began to crumble, sending showers of debris and dust into the air. The very foundation of the monastery seemed to tremble under the weight of their actions. Time seemed to distort as they navigated through the labyrinthine corridors, dodging falling rubble and leaping over cracks in the floor.

Their adrenaline-fueled sprint echoed through the crumbling halls as the sounds of destruction grew louder around them. They could feel the structure giving way beneath their feet, urging them to find an exit before it was too late. The urgency of their escape fueled their determination, propelling them forward despite the chaos and danger that surrounded them.

Finally, with one last burst of energy, Amelia and Milo burst through the grand entrance of the monastery just as the building collapsed behind them. They stumbled out into the open air, their bodies heaving with exhaustion and relief. They turned back to witness the once-majestic monastery reduced to a pile of rubble.

Amelia and Milo stood there, their bodies trembling with a mixture of fear and exhilaration. Nervous laughter escaped their lips as they exchanged glances, unable to fully comprehend the magnitude of their narrow escape. The weight of their journey and the enormity of the task ahead settled upon them, casting a shadow of uncertainty. With trembling hands, they looked down at the black book they had retrieved from the depths of the cavern. Its ancient pages seemed to hold the key to their destiny, a path fraught with danger and darkness. Together, they took a deep breath, their determination resolute.

Chapter Ten

SECRETS OF THE BLACK BOOK

Amelia and Milo hurriedly made their way back to the safety of the old church, seeking solace and a sense of security within its ancient walls. The black book they had retrieved from the collapsing cavern weighed heavily in their hands, its pages filled with cryptic symbols. They knew that within those pages lay the answers they sought, the key to deciphering the clues that would lead them to the ultimate defeat of the Messenger.

Inside the church, they found a quiet corner where the flickering candlelight cast dancing shadows on the weathered stone walls. With the black book laid out before them, Amelia and Milo began their meticulous examination, tracing their fingers over the intricate illustrations and meticulously transcribing the unfamiliar text. It is revealed that only those touched by Fate can read the pages of the book. Hours turned into days as they poured over the pages, their minds consumed by the riddles and secrets hidden within.

Meanwhile, deep below the earth's surface, in the darkness where few dare to tread, the Messenger brooded. Its form, though ethereal, radiated an aura of malevolence. The encounter with Amelia and Milo had left a mark, a crack in its invincibility. For the first time in centuries, fear coursed through its essence. This was a moment of vulnerability, a rare occurrence for a being that had thrived on spreading fear and despair. As the Messenger regained its strength, it felt an unsettling sense of unease.

The Messenger knew it could not let Amelia and Milo succeed in deciphering the clues within the black book. Their determination and resolve posed a threat to its existence, an end to its reign of terror. It concocted a scheme, weaving threads of darkness and deceit to undermine their progress and strike back with a vengeance.

Restless and brooding, the Messenger paced within its underground chamber, surrounded by the remnants of the souls it had taken. They floated as inky blobs, their features distorted and their lips stitched shut, silenced forever. Despite their silent presence, the Messenger could feel their spectral gazes upon it, a constant reminder of its power and the consequences it had wrought.

In the depths of its contemplation, the Messenger began to devise a new plan to strike back at those who dared challenge its reign. It knew that Amelia and Milo were delving into the secrets hidden within the black book, seeking a way to undo the curse that had plagued them. The Messenger's twisted mind concocted a plan to disrupt their progress, to sow doubt and confusion within their hearts.

Within the depths of its hidden lair, the Messenger reveled in its twisted delight as it crafted a malevolent plan to exploit the deepest fears of Amelia and Milo. It knew that true power lay in unraveling the strength within their hearts, and it sought to strike at their vulnerabilities with a ruthless precision.

With the silenced souls floating nearby, their once-peaceful forms now twisted and contorted, the Messenger drew upon their dormant fears, breathing life into their darkest nightmares. It relished in the malicious dance of shadows as the souls transformed into grotesque manifestations of terror, ready to be unleashed upon its unsuspecting victims.

With its cruel laughter echoing in the darkness, the Messenger sent forth these twisted incarnations to infiltrate the minds of Amelia and Milo, each tailored to exploit their unique fears. It relished the thought of their spirits crumbling under the weight of their own vulnerabilities, as doubt and fear gnawed at their courage.

Amelia and Milo immersed themselves in the cryptic contents of the black book, their eyes scanning the ancient text. As they delved deeper into its pages, they stumbled upon a revelation: the knowledge of a specific location that held the key to banishing the Messenger once and for all.

With trembling hands, Amelia traced her fingers over the faded ink, deciphering the intricate details of the ritual. The words spoke of a hidden realm, a place untouched by time, where the boundaries between worlds converged. It was there, in the heart of that mystical location, that the Messenger could be confronted and vanquished.

As Amelia and Milo absorbed the words from the black book, their eyes widened in astonishment. The description of an enigmatic island, erased from maps and shrouded in mystery, captivated their imagination. According to the ancient text, this secluded island held within its depths a structure where Death itself dwelled.

Amelia and Milo, exhausted from their relentless pursuit of knowledge, sought solace within the familiar walls of the old church.

With weariness weighing heavy on their shoulders, Amelia and Milo settled into their makeshift beds, their thoughts lingering on the events that had unfolded. The air was filled with anticipation, as if the world itself held its breath, awaiting the next turn of fate.

As the night settled over Amelia's weary mind, she succumbed to sleep. In the depths of her slumber, the boundaries of reality blurred, and a chilling vision unfolded.

Amelia found herself trapped in a nightmarish realm, where darkness swallowed everything in its path. She stood paralyzed, her heart pounding with dread, as she witnessed a harrowing scene unfold before her eyes. Carlos, her once beloved boyfriend, was subjected to unspeakable torture, his anguished cries piercing the air.

Desperation welled up inside Amelia as she reached out, her voice echoing with futile pleas for help. But her efforts proved in vain, her outstretched hand unable to bridge the insurmountable distance between them. The nightmare taunted her with a cruel reminder of her powerlessness.

Her heart shattered as she watched in horror as Carlos's life was ruthlessly snuffed out, his fate sealed by the merciless hand of her dream's tormentor. The sight of his beheading seared into her mind, etching an indelible mark of sorrow and guilt.

Amelia's breath caught in her throat as Carlos's severed head came to a rest before her, its accusatory gaze fixed upon her trembling form. The whispering voice echoed in her ears, carrying the weight of betrayal and anguish. The question echoed through her mind, piercing her soul with its haunting words: "Why did you do this to me?"

Confusion mingled with horror as Amelia struggled to comprehend the macabre spectacle before her. Her mind raced, desperately seeking answers that eluded her grasp.

Tears welled up in Amelia's eyes as she mustered the strength to respond, her voice quivering with a mix of sorrow and denial. "I didn't do this to you," she whispered, her words laced with anguish. "I would never cause you harm, Carlos. Please, believe me."

Amelia's trembling hands clutched at the dissipating remnants of Carlos's head, only to find them crumbling into dust, slipping through her fingers like memories slipping away. The nightmare that had gripped her so tightly began to unravel, its nightmarish world melting away, leaving Amelia standing alone in an empty void.

Silence enveloped her, broken only by the sound of her own ragged breaths. There was no trace of the nightmare that had haunted her moments ago, no remnants of the accusatory whispers or the spectral presence of Carlos's severed head. It was as if the darkness had swallowed everything, leaving her in a void of emptiness and solitude.

Amelia's gaze darted towards the distant figure that materialized amidst the void. Squinting her eyes, she strained to discern any details in the shape that stood before her. As she approached cautiously, a mixture of trepidation and curiosity coursed through her veins, uncertainty shrouding her every step.

Amelia's heart pounded in her chest as she cautiously approached the figure standing in the distance. As she drew nearer, a knot of unease tightened in her stomach, anticipating what she might find. With each step, the shape began to take form, revealing the figure to be none other than Lily. However, as Lily turned around to face Amelia, a gasp escaped her lips.

Amelia's eyes widened in horror as she beheld Lily's transformed visage. Where once there were vibrant eyes, there were now only empty, hollow sockets staring back at her. The life and light that once resided within Lily had been extinguished, leaving behind an eerie void.

The sight before her was beyond comprehension, a grotesque distortion of her dear friend. Lily's voice pierced the eerie silence, distorted and filled with anguish as she screamed, accusing Amelia of some unfathomable wrongdoing. "Why did you do this to me!" screamed Lily.

Tears streamed down Amelia's face as she recoiled, her mind swirling with confusion and desperation. "Lily, no! I would never..." she choked out, her voice trembling with a mixture of fear and sorrow. But her words fell on deaf ears as Lily lunged at her, driven by a force that seemed to defy logic.

Amelia's screams echoed through the void as she tried to fend off Lily's relentless assault, a mixture of desperation and grief fueling her actions. The once-strong bond of friendship shattered in that moment, replaced by a nightmarish encounter that defied all reason.

Amelia's scream pierced through the void, a raw expression of terror and defiance. She fought with every ounce of strength she could muster, desperately pushing against the distorted figure of Lily. Their struggle became a whirlwind of flailing limbs, filled with frenzied screams and anguished cries.

Amelia awoke from the nightmare, drenched in cold sweat, her breath ragged and trembling. The echoes of Carlos and Lily's cries lingered in her ears, haunting her thoughts and shattering her sense of security. The nightmare's grip tightened around her, threatening to suffocate her spirit.

Tears welled up in Amelia's eyes as she allowed herself a moment of vulnerability. She curled up into a ball, cradling her trembling body in her arms, seeking solace in the embrace of her own vulnerability. Fear lingered in the air, wrapping around her like a suffocating shroud.

As the first rays of morning light filtered through the window, Amelia found herself lost in a profound moment of reflection. She contemplated the depths of her guilt and the haunting images that had plagued her sleep. The weight of her actions and the consequences they had wrought weighed heavily upon her fragile shoulders.

Silent tears continued to flow as Amelia confronted the darkness within her, acknowledging the pain she had caused and the lives that had been irrevocably altered. The realization of her own culpability left her feeling raw and vulnerable, yet it also fueled a fire within her to seek redemption and make amends.

With a deep breath, Amelia resolved to face her fears head-on. She knew that she couldn't undo the past, but she could choose how she moved forward. Determined to find a way to confront the Messenger and unearth the truth that lay hidden, she wiped away her tears and steeled herself for the challenges that lay ahead.

Amelia stepped out of her room and made her way towards the main corridor of the old church. The morning light filtered through the stained-glass windows, casting colorful hues upon the ancient stones.

As she reached the main corridor, Amelia caught sight of Milo standing near one of the tall, arched doorways. His eyes met hers, and she could sense a similar blend of emotions reflected in his gaze. There was an unspoken understanding between them, a shared determination to face the challenges that lay ahead.

Silently, they approached each other, the echoes of their footsteps mingling with the hushed whispers of the sacred space. The weight of their shared journey pressed upon them, and yet there was a sense of camaraderie, a bond forged through adversity.

No words were exchanged at that moment. They didn't need to speak to understand each other. Their presence alone spoke volumes, conveying a mutual resolve to continue their quest and unravel the mysteries that entwined their lives.

Amelia and Milo turned their attention towards the source of the sudden disturbance—an unexpected knock at the front door of the old church. The sound reverberated through the solemn halls, breaking the stillness of their contemplation. They exchanged a quick glance, curiosity and caution mingling in their eyes.

With cautious steps, Amelia and Milo made their way towards the entrance, their hearts pounding in anticipation. As they reached the heavy wooden door, they exchanged a brief moment of silent communication, a shared understanding of the need to proceed with caution.

Milo reached out, his hand hesitating for a moment before grasping the cold iron handle. With a steady push, the door creaked open, revealing a figure standing on the threshold. It was a man, slightly disheveled and bearing a weariness in his eyes.

Chapter Eleven

LOVE BEARING GIFTS

A melia could not believe her eyes, standing before her with a mixture of exhaustion, shame, and relief etched across his features was Carlos. It was a sight she had longed for and feared, unsure of what to expect after their tumultuous past. Emotions surged within her, a whirlwind of confusion and longing.

Amelia's eyes quivered as she stood there, unable to find words to express the myriad of emotions flooding her being. She wanted to embrace him, to feel the warmth of his presence and reassure herself that he was real and standing before her once again.

As Carlos stepped closer, the weight of his absence seemed to hang heavily in the air. There were unspoken questions, wounds that needed tending, and bridges that needed mending. Yet, in that moment, the intensity of their connection superseded all the doubts and uncertainties that had plagued them.

Without a word, Amelia's hand instinctively flew forward, slapping Carlos across the face with a mixture of anger, disbelief, and hurt. The sound of the slap echoed through the church, a sharp punctuation to the charged atmosphere.

Carlos staggered back, his hand instinctively rising to the reddening mark on his cheek. He looked at Amelia with a mixture of shock and remorse, his eyes filled with unspoken words.

Amelia's emotions surged within her, a tumultuous blend of relief, anger, and betrayal. She believed him to be lost forever, and now he stood before her. The conflicting emotions threatened to overwhelm her, and her slap was an impulsive release of pent-up frustration.

Amelia's eyes filled with tears as she struggled to find words. The silence hung heavy in the air, filled with unspoken questions and the weight of their shared history. Carlos, his expression pained, took another step towards her, his voice choked with remorse.

"I'm sorry, Amelia," he whispered, his voice barely audible. "I never meant to hurt you. There were things I didn't understand, things I couldn't explain."

Amelia's anger was replaced by a profound sadness. She wanted to believe him, to understand the reasons behind his absence and the pain it had caused her. But the slap had been an instinctive reaction, a manifestation of her own vulnerability and the wounds that still needed healing.

Amelia's heart wavered between hesitation and of hope as Carlos pleaded for her forgiveness. The conflicting emotions within her churned, torn between the pain of his absence and the longing for what they once had. She gazed into his eyes, searching for sincerity and the love they had shared.

Reluctantly, Amelia found herself slowly lowering her defenses. She understood the weight of regrets, the complexities of human nature. Carlos had returned, seeking redemption, and a part of her still yearned to believe in the possibility of a renewed connection.

"I can't promise that everything will be the same," Amelia finally said, her voice laced with vulnerability. "There's been so much pain and confusion. But I want to believe that we can find a way to heal, to rebuild what was broken."

Carlos nodded earnestly, his eyes brimming with gratitude and a deep sense of regret. "I'll do whatever it takes," he whispered, his voice filled with determination. "I never stopped loving you, Amelia. I'm ready to face the consequences of my actions and make amends."

Carlos and Amelia's embrace was filled with a mixture of relief, vulnerability, and the lingering traces of past affection. In that moment, the weight of their shared history and the trials they had faced seemed to melt away, leaving only the warmth of their connection.

Amelia buried her face in Carlos's chest, seeking solace and reassurance in his embrace. The familiarity of his touch brought a bittersweet comfort, reminding her of the love they had once shared. Carlos held her tightly, his grip conveying a sense of gratitude and remorse, as if he were silently promising to never let her go again.

Amelia began to cry, a culmination of all the pain, longing, and uncertainty that had consumed her in Carlos's absence. As they held each other, the past and present intertwined, mingling hope with the scars of their past. It was a moment of forgiveness, a chance to rewrite their story and build something stronger from the shattered remnants of their relationship.

Carlos's eyes widened as he noticed Milo standing nearby, his presence like an unexpected gust of wind. The tension in the air was palpable as the three of them exchanged wary glances, their individual stories intertwined in a web of uncertainty.

"I see you've made new acquaintances," Carlos remarked cautiously, his voice tinged with curiosity.

Amelia nodded, a hint of unease flickering across her face. "This is Milo," she introduced, gesturing towards him. "He's been helping me with…." Amelia hesitated from saying anything more.

Milo regarded Carlos with a mix of caution and wariness. "Amelia has spoken highly of you," he said, his tone guarded. "But trust is something that must be earned."

Carlos nodded solemnly, understanding the gravity of the situation. "I know I have much to prove," he admitted, his voice tinged with remorse. "But I assure you, I'm committed to doing what's right."

As Carlos shared his journey of searching for Amelia, his words carried a mix of regret and determination. He recounted the moments of despair when he discovered Lily's tragic death and his realization that he had to find Amelia to make things right. "I couldn't bear the thought of losing you too," Carlos confessed, his voice filled with genuine regret. "When I discovered what had happened to Lily, I knew I had to find you."

Amelia listened intently, her emotions in turmoil. She could sense the sincerity in Carlos's voice and saw the genuine remorse etched on his face. Though a part of her still felt the sting of betrayal, another part longed for the connection they once shared. She knew that forgiving Carlos would be a difficult path, but his presence there, in that moment, stirred up conflicting emotions within her.

He explained how he followed the breadcrumbs, asking locals and retracing her steps until he arrived at the old church.

"I never should have left you," Carlos said, his voice filled with regret. "I can't undo the mistakes I made, but I promise you, Amelia, I'm here now, and I will do whatever it takes to make things right."

Amelia's gaze softened as she looked into Carlos's eyes, seeing the vulnerability and sincerity reflected there. The weight of their shared past, the memories and emotions they once cherished, resonated within her. She knew that forgiveness was a complex journey, one that required time and healing, but she also recognized the power of second chances.

Taking a deep breath, Amelia reached out and placed her hand on Carlos's, a silent gesture of tentative reconciliation. "We have a long way to go, Carlos," she said softly, her voice tinged with both caution and hope. "But perhaps, together, we can find the strength to face the Messenger and unravel the secrets that haunt us."

"The Messenger?" Carlos asked with peaked curiosity.

Amelia smiled. "We have a lot of catching up to do."

Amelia took a deep breath and began to recount the events that had transpired since Carlos had left. She spoke of the haunting encounters with the Messenger, the curses, and the relentless pursuit of a way to break free from its grasp.

As she spoke, Carlos listened intently, his expression shifting from surprise to concern.

"I had no idea things had taken such a dark turn," Carlos murmured, remorse evident in his voice. "I'm truly sorry for leaving you to face this alone."

Amelia nodded, her eyes reflecting a mix of sadness and relief. "It was difficult, but I understand why you needed that time away," she replied, her voice softening. "We need all the help we can get to put an end to this curse."

Carlos took a moment to process everything he had heard before finally speaking. "I may not fully comprehend the extent of the danger we face, but I won't turn my back on you again," he said firmly. "We'll find a way to stop the Messenger, together."

Amelia smiled, grateful for Carlos's willingness to stand by her side once more. She knew the challenges ahead would be formidable, but with Carlos's support, they would face them head-on. They embraced, a silent understanding passing between them—a shared commitment to confront their fears and protect each other.

Milo's emotions churned within him as he observed Carlos and Amelia reconnecting. A part of him genuinely felt happiness for Amelia, seeing her find solace and support in Carlos's presence. He knew how much she had missed him and longed for his return. Yet, beneath that happiness, a twinge of jealousy and distrust crept into Milo's heart.

It was difficult for Milo to completely let go of his reservations towards Carlos. He had witnessed the pain and heartbreak Amelia had endured in Carlos's absence. Milo had been there for her, offering his unwavering support and friendship during difficult times. Now, with Carlos's return, a nagging voice inside Milo's mind questioned whether he could truly be trusted.

Milo tried to push those negative thoughts aside, reminding himself that Carlos had apologized and expressed his willingness to help. He knew that unity and cooperation were essential in their mission to confront the Messenger and break the curse. Deep down, Milo wanted to believe that Carlos's intentions were genuine, that he could be a valuable ally in their fight against the darkness.

However, a lingering sense of caution persisted within Milo. He vowed to keep a watchful eye, to protect Amelia and ensure her well-being above all else. It was a delicate balance between embracing their newfound collaboration and maintaining his own reservations. Milo resolved to stay true to his instincts and intuition, allowing time to reveal the true nature of Carlos's intentions.

Amelia and Milo continued to fill Carlos in on their findings about the mysterious Mirage Island, a place where Death itself was said to reside. They explained how their journey had led them to this crucial information, and the significance it held in their quest to banish the Messenger and break the curse once and for all.

Carlos listened intently, his expression a mix of curiosity and concern. He understood the gravity of their mission and the danger they were about to face. Although initially taken aback by the concept of Death residing on an island, he recognized the need to confront this formidable force in order to save themselves and others from the curse's grasp.

"Okay, so let's do it, let's go to this Mirage Island," Carlos said encouragingly, trying his best to accept and support Amelia's claims.

Amelia and Milo exchanged a concerned glance, realizing they were facing a significant hurdle in their quest to reach Mirage Island. Despite all their knowledge and preparations, they had no concrete plan or means to reach this elusive place where Death resided. Uncertainty washed over them, their determination momentarily shaken.

Amelia and Milo found themselves engaged in a heated debate, their voices overlapping as they passionately voiced their differing opinions on how to reach Mirage Island. Tensions ran high as they argued about the best course of action, each stubbornly holding their ground. "I think I might know what to do," Carlos interrupted.

Amelia and Milo turned their attention to Carlos, their expressions a mix of surprise and curiosity. They eagerly awaited Carlos's revelation, hoping that he had stumbled upon a breakthrough that could propel them closer to reaching Mirage Island.

Carlos took a deep breath, collecting his thoughts before speaking. Carlos began recounting his conversation with a weathered captain he met in a bar during his search for Amelia, whose tales of the sea resonated deeply within him. The captain spoke of a forgotten navigational technique passed down through generations of skilled sailors—a method said to reveal hidden paths and guide the way to mythical places.

According to the captain, the technique involved deciphering celestial patterns, aligning with the currents, and paying heed to subtle signs from nature. It required not only keen observation but also a deep connection with the elements and a profound respect for the sea's whims.

As Carlos relayed these details, Amelia and Milo listened intently, their skepticism giving way to a glimmer of hope. Perhaps this forgotten navigational technique held the answers they had been seeking—a way to chart a course to Mirage Island.

Amelia turned to Carlos, her eyes filled with determination. "Do you think you would recognize the captain if we went looking for him?" she asked, her voice brimming with anticipation.

Carlos nodded, a glimmer of excitement in his eyes as he recalled the old captain's weathered face and distinctive seafaring tales. "Absolutely," he replied, his tone filled with certainty. "That old captain left an indelible mark on my memory. I would recognize him anywhere."

Amelia's heart swelled with gratitude, knowing that Carlos's recollection could potentially lead them back to the source of their newfound hope—the key to unlocking the path to Mirage Island. With their resolve renewed, they set off on a quest to find the old captain and embark on their next adventure._

Chapter Twelve

ALL ABOARD

The trio made their way through the bustling streets of the port town, a vibrant tapestry of sights and sounds surrounding them. The salty tang of the sea hung in the air, mingling with the aroma of freshly caught fish and the distant cries of seagulls. The colorful facades of the buildings, weathered by the relentless coastal winds, stood as a testament to the town's long maritime history.

As they walked, Amelia, Carlos, and Milo found themselves immersed in a lively waterfront scene. Sailors hustled and bustled, loading cargo onto ships while exchanging boisterous banter. Wooden fishing boats bobbed gently in the harbor, their worn hulls bearing the marks of countless journeys upon the open seas. The cobbled streets echoed with the rhythmic clatter of footsteps and the occasional distant holler from a vendor, enticing passersby with the promise of freshly caught delicacies.

With determination etched on their faces, the trio approached the weathered locals, their eyes scanning the crowd for any sign of the enigmatic sea captain known as Captain Styx. They engaged in conversations, their inquiries met with nods of recognition and whispers that hinted at the captain's legendary exploits. Stories of treacherous storms, daring rescues, and mysterious encounters with mythical creatures were shared, each tale adding to the lore surrounding the elusive captain.

Time passed, and as the sun began its descent towards the horizon, hope started to wane. Just as the trio was on the verge of despair, a weathered old sailor, his skin bronzed by years of sun and salt, approached them with a knowing smile. "So, you're looking for Captain Styx, are you?" he asked, his voice carrying the weight of countless sea voyages. Excitement surged within them as they nodded eagerly, their eyes fixed on the seasoned sailor. "I might just know where to find him," he said, beckoning them to follow him towards the waterfront.

The trio's footsteps gradually brought them closer to the end of the dock, where a figure stood, silhouetted against the golden hues of the setting sun. The air seemed to hold its breath, anticipation hanging in the space between them and the mysterious individual. As they neared, they could make out the contours of a tall, weathered frame, draped in a long coat that billowed gently in the coastal breeze.

There was an air of quiet authority about the figure, an aura of wisdom and experience that seemed to emanate from every pore. Their features were obscured by the play of shadows, leaving only a hint of a well-defined jawline and piercing eyes that shimmered with a hint of mischief and untold tales. The sound of the lapping waves provided a soothing backdrop to the encounter, amplifying the sense of intrigue that surrounded the enigmatic figure.

As they got closer a soft whistling could be heard seemingly carried by the wind, coming from the man. An all-too-familiar tune that has haunted both Amelia and Milo. They stopped in their tracks, their hearts racing as soon as their minds comprehended what they were hearing. They stared at the figure intensely, instinctively waiting for the horror to begin. Carlos, not understanding why Amelia and Milo froze, followed their leads, trusting their instincts. The whistle stopped, replaced by a deep chuckle. "You look like you have seen a ghost," said the mysterious man mockingly as he turned around stepping into the light.

As the trio came to a stop a few paces away, a knowing smile graced the figure's lips. It was a smile that spoke of adventures lived and challenges overcome, a smile that hinted at the depths of knowledge and secrets held within. The sound of creaking wood underfoot was the only accompaniment to the pregnant pause that enveloped them, until finally, the figure broke the silence.

"Amelia and Milo," the voice carried a melodic timbre, as if each word were imbued with the wisdom of the seas. "I've been expecting you." Glancing over at Carlos, "Now you I did not see coming." A confused but accepting look draped over his eyes. The words hung in the air, their weight sinking deep into the hearts of the trio.

Captain Styx stood tall and commanding, his presence evoking a sense of authority and respect. Weathered lines etched deep into his face, mapping the countless years spent traversing the treacherous seas. His skin, bronzed and weathered by the sun and saltwater, told the story of a life lived amidst the crashing waves and untamed winds.

A cascade of long, salt-and-pepper hair framed his face, flowing like waves frozen in time. Strands of silver danced amidst the dark strands, a testament to the wisdom and experience he carried within. His eyes, the color of the stormy sea, held a captivating intensity that seemed to pierce through the veil of time itself. They shimmered with a mix of mystery and adventure, reflecting the countless tales and secrets that resided within his depths.

Captain Styx was adorned in a long, weathered coat, worn by the elements and time. Its dark fabric billowed gently in the ocean breeze, as if it had absorbed the spirit of the sea itself. Patches and mended seams adorned the coat, a testament to the many battles fought and hardships endured.

In his weathered hands, calloused from years of gripping the helm and working the rigging, Captain Styx held a well-worn compass, its needle pointing steadfastly towards the unknown. Around his neck, a pendant glimmered, depicting a ship navigating treacherous waters, a symbol of his unwavering determination and navigational prowess.

As the trio stood in his presence, they couldn't help but feel a mixture of awe and curiosity. Captain Styx exuded a sense of wisdom and adventure, his very essence intertwined with the vast expanse of the ocean. Amelia and Milo felt a sense of relief wash over them as they observed Captain Styx from a closer distance.

"What do you mean you've been expecting us?" Amelia asked.

Captain Styx chuckled softly, his eyes crinkling at the corners with a hint of amusement. He took a step forward, his weathered boots tapping lightly on the wooden planks of the dock. "Ah, my dear, the sea has its own way of whispering secrets," he replied, his voice carrying a gentle cadence.

Amelia and Milo exchanged puzzled glances, intrigued by the captain's cryptic response. "We've been searching for answers," Milo added, his voice filled with curiosity. "How did you know we would come seeking your guidance?"

Captain Styx's gaze turned towards the distant horizon, as if contemplating the vastness of the ocean itself. "The sea has a way of connecting souls," he said, his voice tinged with a hint of wisdom. "It whispers to those who listen, guiding them to the places they need to be, and the people they need to meet."

He turned his gaze back to Amelia and Milo, his eyes sparkling with a mixture of mystery and understanding. "Your quest has been woven into the very fabric of the ocean's currents. It was only a matter of time before the tides brought you to my shores," he explained, his voice carrying a sense of certainty.

Captain Styx narrowed his eyes as he scrutinized Carlos, his weathered face portraying a mix of curiosity and skepticism. He took a step closer, his presence commanding attention. "And what of you, young man?" he asked, his voice tinged with a hint of suspicion. "What drives you to embark on this perilous journey?"

Carlos met the captain's gaze, his expression resolute. "I stand by Amelia's side," he declared, his voice steady. "I may not possess the same history or knowledge as Amelia and Milo, but I am committed to protecting them and helping them succeed."

A moment of silence hung in the air as Captain Styx studied Carlos intently. The captain's eyes seemed to pierce through Carlos, as if searching for any signs of doubt or wavering resolve. "Devotion is a powerful force, young man," he finally said, his voice carrying a gruff wisdom. "But it is tested in the face of darkness and uncertainty. Are you prepared to face the challenges that lie ahead? To sacrifice when necessary?"

Carlos straightened his posture, determination shining in his eyes. "I am," he responded firmly. "I understand the risks involved, and I am willing to do whatever it takes to protect Amelia and assist in this quest."

A nod of approval crept across Captain Styx's weathered face, a flicker of respect gleaming in his eyes. "Very well," he acknowledged, his voice carrying a hint of acceptance. "Only time will reveal the depths of your devotion, but for now, let us focus on the task at hand. Mirage Island awaits, and we must set sail before the tides turn against us." With that, he turned towards the waiting ship, signaling for the trio to follow.

As the trio approached the looming ship, Milo's footsteps faltered, and his gaze wandered to the tranquil water below. A mixture of anxiety and fear tightened his expression, as if the depths held some deep-rooted dread. Amelia, noticing his sudden hesitation, turned to face him, concern etching her features.

"What's wrong, Milo?" she inquired, her voice filled with genuine worry. Her eyes searched his face, hoping to uncover the source of his unease.

Milo took a deep breath, his hands trembling slightly at his sides. He mustered the courage to meet Amelia's gaze, his eyes filled with vulnerability. "I... I'm terrified of the water," he confessed, his voice tinged with a hint of insecurity.

Amelia's brows furrowed, a mixture of surprise and empathy washing over her. She reached out and gently clasped Milo's trembling hand, offering him a comforting anchor in this moment of vulnerability. "It's all right, Milo," she reassured him, her voice soothing. "We're here for you, and we'll face this challenge together. Trust in yourself, and trust in us."

Milo nodded, gratitude mingling with the lingering fear in his eyes. With Amelia's support, he found the strength to take a step forward, his determination slowly eclipsing his apprehension. The ship awaited them, its deck bathed in the soft glow of the setting sun.

As Captain Styx shouted orders to his crew, the ship's massive sails unfurled, capturing the breeze with a resounding snap. The vessel groaned and creaked, coming alive with the rhythmic motion of the ocean's embrace. Slowly, the ship began to drift away from the safety of the land, carrying the trio into a realm where uncertainty held sway.

Amelia, Milo, and Carlos stood at the ship's railing, their gazes fixed on the receding shoreline. The comforting familiarity of solid ground seemed to taunt them from a distance, a beacon of security that now slipped away. A sense of nostalgia mingled with a pang of trepidation, as they watched the world they knew shrink into a mere speck on the horizon.

The rhythmic lapping of the waves against the hull served as a constant reminder of the vast expanse surrounding them. Each crest and trough whispered tales of unknown depths, where untamed currents and hidden perils lurked. The trio felt a mixture of awe and vulnerability, as the ship sailed further into uncharted waters, leaving behind the safety of the known world.

Amelia's grip tightened on the railing, her knuckles turning pale. She glanced at Milo and Carlos, their expressions mirroring her own mix of anticipation and longing. They shared a silent understanding, a shared acknowledgment of the risks they had willingly embraced. Though their hearts yearned for solid ground, their determination to face the unknown propelled them forward, igniting a flicker of courage in their eyes.

With a final wistful glance towards the fading shoreline, the trio turned their focus to the journey ahead. The ship cut through the restless waves, carving a path towards their destination. Together, they braced themselves for the challenges that awaited, their resolve unwavering as they embraced the unpredictable nature of the open sea.

As the ship sailed further into the vast expanse of the open sea, Milo couldn't help but feel a lingering unease deep within his being. The rhythmic sway of the vessel on the undulating waves stirred conflicting emotions within him, as if his fear of the ocean intertwined with a sense of foreboding that extended beyond the tangible realm.

Milo's unease manifested as a subtle unrest, as though a whisper from the depths of his subconscious was trying to convey a message. He struggled to discern whether it was solely his fear of the vastness of the ocean that unsettled him or if there was something far more ominous lurking beneath the surface.

As he gazed out at the boundless expanse of water, the reflections of sunlight dancing upon the crests of the waves, a shiver ran down Milo's spine. There was a haunting beauty to the sea, its immense power and unknown depths captivating yet unnerving. He couldn't shake the feeling that there was more to his unease than his aversion to water alone, as if an unseen presence stirred within the shadows of his mind.

The unspoken apprehension within Milo wrestled with his rational thoughts, creating an internal struggle that mirrored the vastness of the ocean itself. Deep down, he sensed that his unease held a significance beyond his personal fears, hinting at a connection to the journey they had embarked upon and the dangers that lay ahead. With each passing moment on the ship, Milo's unease grew, a reminder that there was more at stake than his individual worries, and that their quest would demand not only physical resilience, but also the courage to confront the shadows lurking in the depths.

Chapter Thirteen
AN UNEASY SEA

Many nights had gone by since the trio set sail, and the ship resounded with the lively melodies of sea shanties. Carlos and Amelia swayed and spun, their laughter carrying on the ocean breeze as they immersed themselves in the joyous camaraderie of the sailors. Their carefree dance intertwined with the spirited tunes, filling the air with a sense of merriment and respite from their perilous mission.

Amidst the joyful revelry, Milo found himself drawn towards the railing, his gaze fixed on the endless expanse of the rolling sea. While the melodies and the merriment tugged at his spirit, his uneasy feelings lingered like an anchor weighing him down. He watched his companions dancing, their carefree movements and laughter temporarily overshadowing the looming sense of foreboding that gnawed at his heart.

Milo's mind wandered, lost in the ebb and flow of the ocean's rhythm. He couldn't fully immerse himself in the revelry, his thoughts preoccupied with the mysteries that awaited them on Mirage Island and the dark shadows that seemed to lurk just beneath the surface. The sea shanties faded into a distant melody as Milo's introspection took hold, his gaze fixed on the vastness before him.

Captain Styx, ever perceptive, had observed Milo's solitary contemplation from afar. With a knowing smile playing upon his weathered face, the captain stealthily made his way toward the young man, his footsteps softened by the creaking timbers of the ship. As he drew near, he let out a hearty chuckle, causing Milo to startle and look up with surprise.

"Ah, lost in your thoughts, lad?" Captain Styx said, his voice laced with a hint of amusement. His eyes, filled with the wisdom of a seasoned sailor, bore into Milo's troubled gaze, as if peering into the depths of his soul. "What's got you caught in the grip of unease amidst all the merriment?"

Milo hesitated for a moment, his eyes flickering with a mixture of vulnerability and a longing for understanding. Gathering his thoughts, he finally found the courage to voice his concerns to the captain. "It's the water," he admitted, his voice tinged with a hint of apprehension. "I can't help but feel a sense of foreboding, as if something far darker lurks beneath its surface."

Captain Styx's laughter resonated through the night air, as if carrying the weight of countless stories and encounters with the unknown. He placed a weathered hand on Milo's shoulder, his touch firm, yet comforting. "Ah, the sea has a way of stirring up both beauty and fears, young one," he mused. "It reveals truths and secrets that lie hidden from those who dare not venture into its depths. But fear not, for you are not alone in this journey."

Captain Styx, his eyes reflecting the wisdom earned through countless voyages, regarded Milo with a mixture of sympathy and caution. He tightened his grip on Milo's shoulder, his voice carrying a stern yet caring tone. "Beware, lad," he warned. "The ocean is a seductive mistress. Its beauty can enchant, and its fears can consume. But you must not let it pull you too far into its depths, for there lies a darkness that even the bravest of souls struggle to resist."

With a firm, yet gentle, tug, the captain guided Milo away from the railing, leading him back to where Amelia and Carlos stood, their laughter and song filling the air. As they approached, the captain's presence drew the attention of the others, their mirthful expressions giving way to curiosity and concern.

"Ahoy, mates!" Captain Styx called out, his voice cutting through the sounds of the ship. "We have a wary traveler among us, tempted by the mysteries of the sea." His words hung in the air, a reminder of the perils that awaited them. He motioned for Milo to stand beside Amelia and Carlos, his gaze shifting from one face to another, as if silently imparting his unspoken message.

Amelia's eyes sparkled with a mischievous glimmer as she extended her hand towards Milo, her fingers gracefully beckoning him to join her in a dance. Milo's hesitation melted away, and a warm smile curved his lips as he accepted her invitation. The music swirled around them, its lively rhythm guiding their movements with an enchanting grace.

In that moment, the worries that had burdened Milo's heart seemed to fade into the background. He found himself swept up in the joy of the dance, his feet moving in sync with Amelia's, their bodies twirling and spinning as if in perfect harmony. The world around them blurred as they embraced the freedom and exhilaration that the music bestowed upon them.

Meanwhile, Carlos observed from a slight distance, a mix of emotions stirring within him. Jealousy tinged his thoughts, an ache in his heart at witnessing the connection between Milo and Amelia. Yet, there was also a sense of acceptance, recognizing the genuine happiness radiating from both of them. He admired their unity, understanding that Milo had found solace in the dance, and that Amelia had offered him a respite from his inner turmoil.

As the night wore on, the spirited dance gradually transformed into a cozy gathering. The ship's deck became a stage for storytelling, where laughter and camaraderie echoed through the air. Amelia, Milo, Carlos, and Captain Styx settled into a circle amongst the crew, their faces illuminated by the soft glow of lanterns, sharing tales from their lives and adventures.

Amelia's eyes shimmered with enthusiasm as she recounted her childhood escapades, her words painting vivid pictures of daring exploits and wild discoveries. Milo listened intently, captivated by her animated storytelling, his own imagination running wild with images of distant lands and extraordinary encounters.

Carlos, with his charismatic charm, wove tales of daring feats and narrow escapes from his time as a sailor. His narratives were filled with colorful characters and thrilling encounters on stormy seas, evoking a sense of adventure and danger that kept everyone on the edge of their seats.

As the stories flowed, the bond between them grew stronger. They shared laughter, gasps of awe, and moments of quiet reflection. The night seemed to wrap around them like a comforting blanket, creating a sense of warmth and belonging amidst the vast expanse of the sea.

Amelia leaned forward, her eyes sparkling with anticipation, and asked Captain Styx if he would grace them with one of his legendary tales. The captain's weathered face crinkled into a thoughtful expression as he hesitated for a moment, his gaze shifting towards the vast expanse of the night sky.

Finally, with a nod, Captain Styx began his tale, his voice carrying a mix of nostalgia and solemnity. "Long ago..." Amelia, Milo, and Carlos gazed in awe as the old captain began.

"In the heart of a tempestuous storm, the angry waves crashed against the weathered wooden hull of a sailing ship. The howling wind whipped through the rigging, and dark clouds obscured the moon and stars, shrouding the world in an ominous veil. Among the crew, a young sailor clung desperately to the ship's mast, his eyes filled with fear and resignation.

"As the storm raged on, a blinding bolt of lightning split the night sky, illuminating the chaotic scene in a momentary flash. The deafening crack echoed through the air as it struck the ship, tearing it asunder with a violence that seemed to defy nature itself. The young sailor, caught in the fury of the storm, was flung into the churning waters below, the salty spray engulfing him.

"As the sailor fought against the relentless current, his strength waned, and despair began to consume him. With each crashing wave, he was pulled deeper into the watery abyss, his body growing weaker with every passing moment. But amidst the chaos, a sense of serene acceptance washed over him, a surrender to the unforgiving might of the ocean.

"But as if summoned by the sailor's resignation, a figure emerged from the swirling abyss. A radiant being, ethereal and otherworldly, extended a hand toward the drowning sailor. Bathed in a soft, iridescent glow, the figure spoke with a voice that carried both compassion and power. It offered the sailor a choice: to embrace life once more or succumb to the embrace of the unforgiving sea.

"In that moment of surrender, hope surged within the sailor's heart, reigniting his will to survive. With a trembling hand, he reached out and grasped the outstretched hand of the mysterious figure.

"As the sailor's consciousness faded into the depths of darkness, the cacophony of crashing waves and roaring winds faded away, replaced by a profound stillness. Time passed unnoticed, and when he finally regained awareness, he found himself in a world transformed. Opening his eyes, he beheld the sight of a deserted island, its shores kissed by gentle waves and framed by swaying palm trees.

"The air was thick with the fragrance of tropical blooms, a symphony of vibrant colors painting the landscape. Sunlight filtered through the verdant canopy overhead, casting dappled patterns on the soft, golden sand beneath his bare feet. The sailor felt the warmth of the sun's embrace on his skin, a gentle reminder of the fragile beauty that surrounded him.

"Curiosity tugged at the sailor's adventurous spirit as he approached the center of the island. There, nestled amidst the verdant foliage, stood a structure that seemed to beckon him closer. Its weathered stones whispered tales of ancient secrets, and the sailor's heart quickened with anticipation. He stepped into the dimly lit chamber, and a sense of awe washed over him as he beheld the carvings etched into the walls.

"The carvings told a story of grand proportions, a battle of mythical beings whose colossal forms clashed amidst swirling tempests and celestial fires. The intricately carved figures seemed to come to life, their fierce expressions frozen in eternal struggle. Each stroke of the chisel revealed the raw power and raw emotions of the combatants, capturing a clash of titans that echoed through the annals of time.

"As the sailor traced his fingers along the ancient engravings, he felt a connection to the long-forgotten tale. The images danced before his eyes, evoking a sense of primal energy and ancient wisdom. He marveled at the craftsmanship, the attention to detail that rendered every sinew and scale, every weapon and gesture, with striking realism. The artist's skill breathed life into the stone, as if the battle itself had been etched into the very fabric of the universe.

"The sailor's reverie was abruptly shattered by a soft, melodic voice that seemed to drift through the chamber, resonating with otherworldly grace. It called out to him, piercing the stillness with its ethereal cadence. Startled, the sailor turned, his gaze drawn to the source of the enchanting sound.

"There, standing before him, bathed in a faint glow, was the figure that had saved him from the clutches of the tempestuous sea. The beauty and grace emanating from this otherworldly being captivated his senses, as if a fragment of celestial radiance had taken on human form.

"The figure's eyes sparkled with an ancient wisdom, reflecting the eons of knowledge they had acquired. A serene smile played upon lips that held the secrets of countless ages. The sailor found himself entranced by the figure's presence, his heart filled with an inexplicable mix of gratitude and curiosity.

"With a voice that echoed with the whisper of ocean waves and the song of the wind, the figure spoke to the sailor. Its words carried a weight of power and purpose, resonating deep within his soul.

"As the echoes of the figure's voice settled, a solemn air enveloped the chamber, and the sailor's heart sank. The being's gaze pierced through him, its eyes filled with a mix of compassion and expectation. The realization dawned upon the sailor that his survival came at a price, a debt to be repaid in service to this enigmatic entity.

"As the sailor defiantly refused the being's request, a chilling breeze swept through the chamber, carrying an undercurrent of icy determination. In that instant, the air around him seemed to grow heavy, his breath constricted, and panic coursed through his veins. As if fate itself had conspired against him, the very essence of life began to slip from his grasp.

"In a cruel twist of fate, his lungs betrayed him, and the taste of saltwater invaded his mouth once more. As his body convulsed and his vision blurred, he realized that his defiance had dire consequences. The weight of his decision pressed upon him like an anchor, dragging him deeper into the depths of the ocean's abyss.

"As the darkness threatened to claim him, a voice, tinged with both sorrow and resolve, resounded within his mind. It was the voice of the being, a bittersweet melody that cut through the suffocating silence. The voice reminded him of the fragile nature of his existence, the precarious balance between life and death, and the choices that could shape his destiny.

"As the sailor, with a heavy heart and a hint of resignation, yielded to the demand of the enigmatic being, a peculiar stillness settled upon the chamber. The water that had threatened to consume him receded, its suffocating grasp relinquished. A profound calm washed over his being, replacing the frantic struggle with a newfound clarity.

"With a voice that echoed both ancient wisdom and an untold burden, the being responded to the sailor's surrender. Its words carried a weight that transcended the confines of the chamber, resonating deep within his soul. It revealed the purpose that had been woven into the fabric of his existence, a task of paramount importance that only he could fulfill.

"The sailor, now bound by destiny's intricate threads, felt a mixture of trepidation and resolve as he posed the question that hung in the air like a delicate mist. He inquired, with a voice filled with earnestness, about the nature of his newfound purpose and the path he must embark upon. The answer, wrapped in enigmatic words and mysterious prophecies, unfolded before him like a tapestry of hidden truths.

"With his destiny intertwined with the fateful being, the sailor found himself bestowed with a solemn duty that transcended the boundaries of mortal existence. He became the ferryman of lost souls, entrusted with the task of guiding those who perished at sea to the realm of judgment. No longer a mere mortal, he walked the threshold between worlds, straddling the realms of the living and the dead.

"Under the moonlit skies, he embarked on his ethereal vessel, gliding silently through the midnight waters. The souls of the departed, adrift and disoriented, were drawn to the beckoning presence of the sailor. They emerged from the depths, their spectral forms shimmering with an otherworldly glow. Some approached with expressions of sorrow, others with a lingering sense of longing, while a few bore the weight of their regrets.

"With compassionate eyes, the sailor welcomed each lost soul, offering solace and guidance in their final journey. He listened to their stories, their whispered regrets and unfulfilled dreams, as they sought redemption and closure. With a touch as gentle as a sea breeze, he ushered them into the boat, their ethereal essence mingling with the salty air.

"Navigating the realm of the departed, the sailor guided the vessel toward the shores of destiny. A realm beyond mortal comprehension awaited, where the souls would face their judgment, their deeds weighed upon the scales of justice. Through treacherous tides and uncharted currents, he sailed with unwavering determination, honoring the weighty responsibility that had been bestowed upon him."

Silence hung heavy in the air as the echoes of the captain's haunting tale reverberated within the hearts of Amelia, Milo, and Carlos. The weight of the story pressed upon their shoulders, rendering them speechless, their minds consumed by the enigmatic realm of the supernatural. Time seemed to stand still as they processed the profound implications of the narrative, their thoughts swirling in a whirlpool of uncertainty and awe.

Breaking the tension, a deep chuckle rumbled from the captain's chest, dissipating the lingering unease. His eyes twinkled mischievously, cutting through the solemn atmosphere like a ray of sunlight piercing through stormy clouds. With a knowing smile, he reassured the trio that it was merely a tale spun from the fabric of imagination, a yarn spun to captivate and enthrall.

His hearty laughter danced upon the breeze, carrying with it a sense of relief and camaraderie. The captain, with his weathered features and salt-tinged beard, exuded an air of wisdom and a touch of playfulness. He had seen countless sailors come and go, their hearts burdened by the mysteries of the sea, and he understood the impact that stories could have on the vulnerable human psyche.

As the echoes of the captain's laughter subsided, a newfound lightness permeated the air. The trio exchanged glances, the weight of the story lifted from their shoulders, replaced by a shared sense of wonder and amusement. Though the tale had momentarily gripped them in its spectral embrace, they now found solace in the realization that it was but a figment of imagination, a creation meant to stir the depths of their souls.

With a wink and a nod, the captain urged them to release the tendrils of fear and uncertainty that had taken hold. He reminded them that they were bound for an adventure of their own making, guided not by the supernatural realms of folklore, but by their own resolve and camaraderie. The story, while captivating, was merely a fleeting moment in the grand tapestry of their journey, a reminder to cherish each step and to embrace the unknown with courage and resilience.

The captain, his face now etched with a touch of seriousness, raised a weathered hand and beckoned the trio to follow. With a brisk nod, he gestured toward the cabins below deck, urging them to seek rest and respite. The time for contemplation and storytelling had come to an end, giving way to the practicalities of the voyage.

As they made their way through the dimly lit corridors of the ship, the captain's sturdy boots echoed against the wooden floorboards, a rhythmic reminder of the ship's ceaseless movement upon the waves. His stride was purposeful, guiding them with an air of authority that spoke of years spent traversing the treacherous seas.

The flickering lanterns cast elongated shadows that danced along the passageways, creating an ethereal ambiance that enveloped the weary travelers. The gentle creaking of the ship, as if it were whispering secrets to the night, provided a soothing backdrop to their steps.

Reaching the threshold of their respective cabins, the captain halted and turned to face Amelia, Milo, and Carlos. His eyes, glinting with a mixture of warmth and command, met each of theirs in turn. He offered a reassuring smile, a silent reassurance that they were safe under his watchful gaze.

"Rest well, my friends," he said in a voice that carried both authority and compassion. "Tomorrow holds its own challenges and wonders. The sea has a way of revealing both, in due time."

With those parting words, the captain bid them goodnight, his figure disappearing into the shadows of the ship's interior. As the trio entered their cabins, a sense of weariness mingled with a flicker of anticipation. The rhythmic lullaby of the ship's movements lulled them into a state of drowsiness, promising respite and renewal.

In the cozy embrace of their cabins, the world outside seemed to fade away. The air was filled with a subtle scent of salt and adventure, their dreams interwoven with the mysteries that lay beyond the horizon. The captain's guidance echoed in their thoughts, a gentle reminder to surrender to the embrace of sleep, for the challenges of the morrow awaited them with open arms.

With a final sigh, they surrendered to the call of rest, knowing that tomorrow held new chapters to be written, and that their spirits would awaken, replenished and ready to face the ever-unfolding story of their shared journey.

Chapter Fourteen
There's Something in the Water

A soft breeze whispered through the cracks in the cabin walls, carrying with it an eerie voice that seemed to originate from somewhere beyond the veil of dreams. It echoed in his ears, a haunting plea that permeated the air. The voice was both familiar and foreign, like a distant echo from a long-forgotten memory.

"Wake up," it whispered, each syllable tinged with urgency. "Wake up...wake up..."

The voice persisted, its pleading tone growing more desperate with each repetition. Milo's brow furrowed, his mind grasping at the elusive strands of understanding. Was this a mere figment of his imagination, or a message from a realm beyond their own?

Milo lay there, fully awake now, his senses acutely attuned to the shifting ambiance around him. The stillness in the air was broken by the ominous sound of a single drop of water, striking his forehead with a chilling touch. His eyes followed the path of the droplet as it traced a line down his face, eventually dripping onto his fingertip. Mesmerized by this tiny, transient bead, his gaze became fixated on its surface, as if it held the secrets of the universe within its form.

But before he could fully grasp the significance of this minuscule droplet, the ship convulsed violently, as if seized by unseen hands. The sudden, jarring motion threw Milo off balance, propelling him across the cabin floor with an unexpected force. His body collided with the unforgiving surface, causing a dull ache to radiate through his limbs.

As he lay sprawled on the floor, the ship continued to tremble beneath him, its wooden structure creaking and groaning in protest. The once-familiar surroundings now felt unsteady and treacherous, their stability eroded by the volatile dance of the sea. Milo's heart raced, his mind filled with a maelstrom of fear and confusion.

He struggled to regain his footing, using the furniture as makeshift support in the tumultuous environment. With each surge and sway of the ship, his body fought against the disorienting currents, desperately seeking balance amidst the chaos. As he steadied himself, his thoughts turned to his companions, wondering if they too were experiencing the harrowing turbulence that threatened to consume them all.

Gathering his resolve, Milo braced himself against the relentless surges of the ship, his determination to protect and survive fueling his actions. The relentless onslaught of the tempest raged outside, matching the tempest that now churned within his very being.

Milo emerged from his cabin, his senses on high alert, only to collide abruptly with Amelia and Carlos, who stood just outside his door, their expressions etched with worry and panic. Their eyes met, and in that instant, they understood that they were all caught in the same tempest of fear and uncertainty.

Amelia's usually composed demeanor was replaced by a furrowed brow and a sense of urgency in her voice. She clutched a nearby railing for support, her fingers gripping it tightly as if holding onto the last vestiges of stability. Carlos, typically calm and collected, appeared disheveled, his hair tousled and his normally steady hands trembling slightly.

Their breaths came in shallow gasps, their chests rising and falling with an anxious rhythm. It was as if the very air around them crackled with an unseen tension, amplifying their unease. Their shared silence spoke volumes, conveying the gravity of the situation without the need for words.

Milo pushed open the door to his cabin, stepping out into the narrow corridor, only to find Amelia and Carlos already there, their expressions etched with deep concern. Panic radiated through the air, casting a palpable tension that hung heavy upon them all. Without uttering a single word, their eyes met, silently acknowledging the urgency of the situation that bound them together.

In unison, they instinctively knew that seeking the refuge of the upper deck was their only chance for survival amidst the growing turmoil. They moved swiftly, their footsteps echoing through the dimly lit passageways, each step accompanied by the rumbling growl of thunder that reverberated through the vessel.

As they emerged onto the upper deck, a breathtaking scene unfolded before their eyes. The skies were ablaze with otherworldly luminosity, streaks of jagged lightning crackling across the heavens, illuminating the night with an eerie, otherworldly glow. Waves crashed against the sides of the ship with a ferocity that sent shivers down their spines, their towering crests threatening to engulf the fragile vessel in an instant.

The wind howled with a relentless fury, whipping through their hair and clothes, as if possessed by some unseen force. The air itself seemed to vibrate with a palpable energy, charged with an electric intensity that prickled against their skin. Above them, dark clouds churned and twisted, a tempestuous ballet of chaos and power.

In the face of this awe-inspiring yet terrifying spectacle, the trio stood transfixed, their eyes wide with a mixture of awe and trepidation. Nature had unleashed its fury upon them, a display of its immense might and merciless unpredictability. They knew they had entered a realm beyond their control, a realm where survival would depend on their resilience and resourcefulness.

Amidst the chaos of the storm, the trio's attention was drawn to the frenetic flurry of activity taking place around them. The crew members, their faces etched with determination and beads of sweat and rain glistening on their brows, moved with purpose and urgency. They scurried along the rain-soaked deck, their footsteps slipping and sliding against the wet wooden planks as they carried out their assigned tasks with unwavering focus.

The captain stood steadfast at the helm, his commanding presence a beacon of stability amidst the tempestuous sea. His voice, strong and unwavering, cut through the howling wind, issuing orders that echoed across the deck. Each command was met with a flurry of responses, as crew members raced to carry out his instructions, their movements synchronized with practiced precision.

Ropes were pulled taut, sails were adjusted with deftness, and rigging was secured against the relentless onslaught of the storm. The ship groaned under the strain, creaking and lurching with each monstrous wave that crashed against its hull. Yet, the crew worked with unwavering determination, their collective efforts a testament to their skill and experience in navigating treacherous waters.

Amidst the cacophony of roaring winds and crashing waves, the sound of the captain's voice pierced through the turmoil, a steady and unwavering beacon of guidance. His words carried authority and assurance, instilling a sense of trust and confidence in the hearts of those under his command. He stood tall, his eyes fixed on the horizon, as if locked in a fierce battle of wills with the very elements themselves.

"Amelia! Milo! Carlos!" Captain Styx's voice boomed over the storm, cutting through the chaos like a thunderclap. His voice carried a mix of urgency and authority, demanding the trio's attention.

Amelia turned to face the captain, rain cascading down her face as she squinted through the driving rain. "Captain Styx, what's happening? Is the ship going to be okay?"

The captain's stern expression softened slightly as he met Amelia's gaze. "Hold on tight, lass. We're facing a fierce storm, but fear not, we've weathered worse. We'll see this through together."

Milo, his voice filled with concern, interjected, "But Captain, the storm seems relentless. Is there any way we can navigate around it?"

Captain Styx raised an eyebrow, his eyes fixed on the tumultuous sea ahead. "I've sailed these treacherous waters for years, lad. Trust me when I say there's no escaping the clutches of this storm. Our only option is to face it head-on and pray for calmer seas on the other side."

Carlos, his voice filled with a mixture of determination and worry, chimed in. "What can we do to help, Captain? We're not seasoned sailors, but we're willing to lend a hand."

The captain's eyes narrowed, his gaze shifting from one face to another. "Listen closely, all of you. Find something to hold onto and brace yourselves. This storm won't break our spirit. We'll fight tooth and nail to keep this ship afloat. Stay strong, trust your instincts, and follow my lead. Together, we'll defy the fury of the sea."

The captain's gaze flickered momentarily towards the churning waters below, and Milo followed his line of sight. There, beneath the surface of the inky abyss, a shadowy presence seemed to stir. The water rippled and swirled, disturbed by the unseen force that lurked within.

Milo's breath caught in his throat as he strained his eyes, attempting to discern the nature of the mysterious creature that moved with stealth beneath the tumultuous surface. The shadow shifted and undulated, its form elusive and enigmatic. It was massive, dwarfing the ship in comparison, its true magnitude hidden beneath the veil of darkness.

The captain's voice, tinged with a mix of concern and authority, pulled Milo's attention back to the urgent present.

He watched as the captain barked orders to the crew, directing their efforts towards steering the ship away from the unseen menace lurking below. The sailors scrambled to adjust the course, their movements infused with a sense of urgency and purpose.

As the ship veered away from the shadowy depths, Milo's eyes remained fixed on the turbulent waters. He couldn't shake the feeling of being watched, of unseen eyes scrutinizing their every move. The enormity of the creature, both awe-inspiring and fearsome, sent a shiver down his spine. What lay beneath those dark depths? What secrets did the mysterious shadow hold?

The trio huddled together, their bodies tense with anticipation and uncertainty. The captain's words, filled with both caution and determination, echoed in their ears, urging them to stay vigilant.

The ship groaned and shuddered, its wooden frame straining under the unexpected force that abruptly brought it to a halt. The sudden cessation of motion sent a jolt through the vessel, causing the trio and the crew to stumble and crash to the floor, their bodies colliding with the unforgiving planks.

Amelia, Carlos, and Milo found themselves sprawled on the deck, disoriented and bewildered by the unforeseen disruption. The air was thick with a mixture of confusion and anxiety as they struggled to regain their footing, their senses attuned to the disconcerting stillness that enveloped the ship.

Milo's heart raced within his chest as he cast his eyes around, trying to make sense of the situation. The once-ferocious storm still brewing, yet somehow the ship seemed frozen in time. The creaking of the ship's timbers, strained under the weight of the mysterious force that held it captive, reverberated through the silence.

As the trio rose to their feet, their movements cautious and tentative, they exchanged worried glances. The crew members scrambled to their feet, their expressions a mix of fear and determination. The captain's voice rang out, commanding authority and resilience as he rallied his crew, urging them to stay vigilant and prepare for whatever awaited them.

As the ship lay trapped in the grip of the unknown, an eerie melody drifted through the air, echoing from the depths of the vessel. The haunting sound filled the corridors, captivating the senses of all who heard it. The instruments, long dormant and untouched, sprang to life, their strings resonating with a spectral touch.

Amelia's eyes widened as the familiar tune reached her ears. It was the same melody that had emanated from the mysterious music box, filling her heart with both nostalgia and unease. Milo's gaze met Amelia's, their eyes mirroring a mixture of astonishment and apprehension.

As the haunting melody filled the air, an insidious voice reverberated through the ship, its sinister presence palpable. It slithered through the corridors, weaving its way into the minds of Amelia, Milo, and Carlos.

"So close," the insidious voice reverberated through the air, its malevolent tone sending shivers down the spines of the trio. "This ship is mine, and its crew will die because of you," it whispered, its words dripping with dark delight.

Amelia's eyes widened in terror as she watched the scene unfold before her. Black tendrils, like writhing serpents, slithered through the air, their wicked touch snatching the unsuspecting sailors one by one. Panic ensued, cries of fear and desperation echoing through the ship as the crew fought against the ethereal assailants.

Captain Styx's commanding voice, resolute and unwavering. "Come to me, quickly!" he called out, his words carrying a sense of urgency.

Amelia, Milo, and Carlos exchanged determined glances, their eyes filled with both fear and trust. Without hesitation, they moved towards the captain, fighting against the encroaching darkness that swallowed the ship.

As they reached Captain Styx's side, they watched in horror as the crew members were snatched away, vanishing into the clutches of the malevolent force. The trio stood shoulder to shoulder, their hearts pounding in their chests.

The piercing screams and desperate cries of the sailors echoed through the air, a haunting chorus that sent shivers down the spines of Amelia, Milo, Carlos, and Captain Styx. Each wail carried with it a mixture of fear, agony, and despair, filling the air with an overwhelming sense of anguish.

Amelia's voice trembled with urgency as she asked the question that lingered on everyone's minds, "What do we do now?" The group huddled together, their minds racing, desperately trying to devise a plan amidst the chaos that surrounded them.

Carlos's voice broke through the tension, his words laced with determination. "We need to find a way to fight back. There must be something on this ship that can help us."

Amelia nodded, her eyes scanning their surroundings for any sign of salvation. "We should search for weapons or anything that can be used as a defense. We can't let fear paralyze us."

As they were discussing their next move, a slithering, black tendril emerged from the shadows, snaking its way towards Milo. The air grew heavy with dread as the tendril coiled around his ankle, its grip tightening with every passing moment.

Milo's voice trembled with fear as he shouted, "Help me! It's got me!"

Amelia and Carlos stood frozen in terror as the black tendril wrapped tightly around Milo's ankle, its grip unyielding and merciless. Panic surged through their veins, leaving them momentarily paralyzed as they watched their friend being dragged perilously closer to the edge of the ship.

"No! Milo!" Amelia's voice cracked with desperation, her eyes wide with horror. "We have to do something!"

Carlos's voice trembled as he shouted, "Hang on, Milo!"

As Milo teetered perilously close to the edge of the ship, his fingers slipping from Amelia's desperate grasp, Carlos's instincts kicked in. Without a second thought, he lunged forward, his body diving through the air towards his friend. With a surge of strength, he managed to seize Milo's outstretched hand just as he was about to be consumed by the darkness.

"Carlos!" Amelia's cry of relief mingled with her astonishment.

Carlos grunted, his face etched with determination as he tightened his grip on Milo's hand. "I won't let go, Milo!"

As Amelia and the captain rushed to Carlos and Milo's side, their hearts pounding with a mix of urgency and fear, another tendril emerged from the darkness, snaking its way towards the captain. In a split second, it wrapped around his leg with a vice-like grip, pulling him away from the group.

"Captain!" Amelia cried out, her voice filled with desperation.

Carlos, still holding onto Milo, instinctively reached out towards the captain. "Hold on, Captain!"

The captain, his face a mask of determination, fought against the encroaching darkness, straining against the pull of the tendril. "Save yourselves," he grunted through gritted teeth. "Find a way to stop this."

Carlos, his voice filled with determination and concern, turned to Amelia and urgently said, "Go, Amelia! Help the Captain!"

Amelia's eyes widened with a mix of worry and determination as she nodded in agreement. With a deep breath, she turned on her heels and rushed towards the captain, her heart pounding in her chest. As she reached out for the captain's outstretched hand, the tendril tightened its grip, threatening to pull him over the edge of the ship.

"Captain, hold on! I've got you!" Amelia shouted, her voice filled with a fierce resolve.

The captain, his face etched with pain, strained against the relentless pull of the tendril. "Amelia, go! Save yourself!" he urged, his voice laced with concern.

Carlos, his heart pounding with determination, strained against the relentless force of the black tendrils that coiled around Milo's body, constricting tightly around his throat. Desperation laced his voice as he shouted, "Milo, don't let go! I won't let it take you!"

Milo gasped for air, his face turning pale as the tendrils tightened their grip. He struggled to hold on, his strength fading rapidly. "Carlos, I can't... I can't breathe..."

Carlos's hands trembled as he fought against the overwhelming force, his muscles strained with the weight of his friend's life hanging in the balance. "Milo, please... Hold on just a little longer!"

Milo's gaze locked with Carlos's, a flicker of understanding and acceptance passing between them. Carlos pleaded, his voice cracking with desperation, "Milo, please... Don't let go! Hold on!"

But Milo's strength waned, his body growing limp as the tendrils tightened their grip. With a pained smile, he whispered, his voice barely audible, "Carlos... it's okay. Take care of her...."

Tears streamed down Carlos's face as he clung to Milo's hand, his grip slipping against the relentless force of the tendrils. "No, Milo! I won't let you go! Stay with me!"

Milo's grip weakened, his hand slipping through Carlos's desperate fingers. He offered one last feeble smile before being forcefully dragged into the unforgiving depths of the sea. Carlos's anguished cry echoed through the stormy night.

Carlos's anguish hung heavy in the air, his heart shattered by the loss of Milo. But in that moment of darkness, a cry for help pierced through the chaos, slicing through his despair. His head snapped towards the sound, his eyes widening with fear. "Amelia!"

Without a moment's hesitation, Carlos sprinted across the ship, his feet pounding against the rain-soaked deck. With each step, his heart pounded in sync with his rapid breaths.

He could see Amelia, her form ensnared by the insidious tendrils that threatened to drag her into the depths below.

"Amelia!" Carlos's voice resounded with urgency, his tone filled with a fierce determination. He reached out towards her, his hand yearning to grasp hers and pull her to safety. "Hold on, Amelia! I'm coming!"

The world around Carlos seemed to blur as he witnessed Amelia and the captain being forcefully yanked through the weakened wooden railing, the sound of splintering wood echoing through the tumultuous storm. A surge of adrenaline surged through his veins, overriding any sense of self-preservation. Without a second thought, Carlos propelled himself forward, his body slicing through the air as he dived into the churning waters below.

Amidst the crashing waves, Carlos fought against the strong currents that threatened to pull him away from Amelia's fading form. "Amelia!" he yelled, his voice battling against the howling winds. "Hold on! I'm coming for you!"

The salty water engulfed him, its icy grip biting at his skin. But Carlos pressed forward, his heart fueled by determination and love. He swam with all his might, propelling his body through the roiling sea, his eyes fixed on the spot where Amelia had disappeared.

As Carlos desperately searched the tumultuous waters for any sign of Amelia, his strength waned, and exhaustion seeped into his bones. The weight of his failure bore down upon him, his heart heavy with the crushing realization that he may not be able to save her. "Amelia, where are you?" he called out, his voice laced with desperation, but his words were swallowed by the roaring wind and crashing waves.

His limbs grew heavy, and the frigid water seemed to envelop him, pulling him deeper into the unfathomable depths. Carlos felt his body sinking, his energy depleting with each passing moment. Doubt and self-blame gnawed at his spirit, threatening to consume him entirely.

"I tried... I'm sorry, Amelia," he murmured, his voice a mere whisper carried away by the currents. In that moment of surrender, Carlos let go of the fight, accepting the cruel fate that awaited him. The darkness of the ocean closed in around him, enveloping him in its icy embrace.

As Carlos teetered on the brink of death, his body weary and his hope waning, a sudden glimmer of light pierced through the stormy chaos. Before him, a figure emerged from the murky depths, ethereal and radiant, an embodiment of both beauty and enigma. The being's presence commanded attention, and Carlos found himself captivated by its otherworldly allure.

"Desperate souls seek solace in the depths," the being whispered, its voice a melodic harmony that resonated within Carlos's core. "I can offer you a choice, a chance to save your friends at the cost of your own life. Do you accept?"

Carlos's breath hitched, his heart pounding with both trepidation and an unwavering resolve. He gazed into the depths of the being's eyes, seeing within them a glimmer of hope, a path to redemption. Without hesitation, he mustered the strength to speak, his voice filled with a mix of determination and selflessness.

"Yes," he replied, his voice firm and resolute. "I will trade my life for theirs. Please, save them."

The being nodded, its form shimmering with an otherworldly glow. Carlos could feel the weight of the decision settling upon him, the gravity of sacrificing his own existence to preserve the lives of those he held dear. Yet, in his heart, he knew it was the only choice, the ultimate act of love and sacrifice.

As the storm raged on, the tempestuous waves crashing against the ship, a blinding flash of light erupted from the churning sea. In an instant, the world transformed.

As Amelia and Milo regained consciousness on the sandy shore, they coughed up water, disoriented and bewildered by their sudden arrival. Relief flooded through Amelia and Milo as they looked at each other, their eyes filled with a mix of disbelief and joy. "We're okay!" Amelia exclaimed, her voice brimming with elation. Milo echoed her sentiment, his voice carrying the weight of their survival.

However, their elation was abruptly tempered as Amelia's gaze shifted towards Captain Styx, who stood a few paces away, his expression grave and contemplative. Sensing something amiss, Amelia approached him, her voice laced with concern. "What's wrong, Captain?" she asked, her tone tinged with worry.

The captain turned to face Amelia, his eyes reflecting a depth of sorrow and understanding. He let out a heavy sigh before finally speaking, his voice tinged with a mix of grief and acceptance. "Haven't you noticed yet?" he questioned, his words hanging in the air, heavy with an unspoken truth.

Confusion creased Amelia's brow as she turned her gaze toward the vast expanse of the sea, its waves crashing against the shore. And then it hit her like a torrential wave. Carlos was nowhere to be found. The realization created a pang of emptiness settling in her chest.

Amelia, overcome with grief and longing, frantically paced along the beach, her voice filled with desperate calls for Carlos. "Carlos! Carlos, where are you?" she cried out, her voice echoing through the air. Each step she took was fueled by a desperate hope, as if she could summon him back with her sheer determination.

However, Captain Styx, a somber presence standing nearby, approached Amelia, his voice carrying a solemn tone. "Amelia," he interjected gently, his words laced with empathy, "it's no use. Carlos is not here. He's... gone." His voice trailed off, a heavy sigh escaping his lips.

Amelia's voice trembled with desperation as she pleaded with Captain Styx, her eyes filled with tears. "Captain, please tell me where Carlos is. Why isn't he here with us? We have to find him," she implored, her words carrying a mix of anguish and hope.

The captain's gaze softened as he met Amelia's eyes, his voice calm but tinged with sorrow. "Amelia, it is no coincidence that we have arrived safely on this beach while Carlos did not," he explained gently, his voice carrying the weight of the truth he was about to reveal. "Carlos made a selfless sacrifice for our sake. He chose to stay behind, to face the darkness and ensure our escape."

Amelia's breath caught in her throat as the captain's words sank in. Her mind struggled to comprehend the depth of Carlos's sacrifice, the magnitude of his bravery. A flood of emotions washed over her—gratitude, guilt, and a profound sense of loss.

Amelia's heart ached with grief as she struggled to come to terms with the weight of Carlos's sacrifice. Tears streamed down her face as she whispered through her sobs, "Carlos, you promised... you promised you wouldn't leave again."

The captain, with a gentle understanding in his eyes, stepped forward, placing a comforting hand on Amelia's shoulder. "Amelia, I know this is incredibly difficult for you," he said, his voice filled with compassion. "But Carlos's sacrifice was not in vain. Look over there."

Amelia lifted her tear-stained gaze and followed the captain's pointed finger. There, in the distance, amidst the crashing waves and shrouded in an ethereal mist, stood Mirage Island—the place they had long sought, the place where legends claimed death resided.

"We're here, Amelia. We have arrived at Mirage Island," the captain declared, his voice filled with a mix of determination and awe.

Amelia's tearful eyes widened as a surge of anticipation and resolve replaced her grief. Mirage Island, the fabled destination of their perilous journey, was finally within their reach. She could almost feel the weight of its mysteries and secrets calling out to her, beckoning her forward.

Amidst her sorrow, Amelia felt a flicker of hope ignite within her. Carlos's sacrifice, as painful as it was, had led them to this pivotal moment. It was a reminder that their mission, their pursuit of the truth, held profound significance.

Amelia wiped away her tears, her voice trembling but filled with newfound determination. "We will honor Carlos's sacrifice, Captain. We will uncover the truth that awaits us on Mirage Island," she declared, her voice filled with a blend of sorrow and unwavering resolve.

The captain nodded, a solemn expression on his face.

"Indeed, Amelia. We will continue our journey, carrying Carlos's memory in our hearts, and we will face whatever challenges await us on this island," he affirmed, his voice tinged with a steely resolve._

Chapter Fifteen
To the Heart of the Island

Amelia, Milo, and Captain Styx forged ahead through the mysterious and treacherous terrain of Mirage Island. The atmosphere was heavy with an otherworldly presence, the air tinged with a mix of anticipation and unease. Each step seemed to echo with a profound sense of purpose and the weight of their individual journeys.

Amelia's heart remained burdened with the loss of Carlos. Amelia's tear-streaked face was a constant reminder of the loss they had endured, and her sorrow weighed heavily upon her heart. Though her determination pushed her forward, a shadow of sadness lingered in her eyes. She couldn't shake the feeling of his absence, the void that he had left behind. "Carlos... I wish you were here with us," she whispered, her voice tinged with longing.

Milo, on the other hand, found himself grappling with a whirlwind of emotions. Surviving the ordeal at sea and witnessing the sacrifices made by Carlos had left him questioning his own existence. His mind raced with a multitude of thoughts, trying to comprehend the fragility of life and the purpose behind his miraculous escape. "I can't believe I made it through... It feels like a second chance," he murmured, his voice filled with a mixture of gratitude and confusion.

Meanwhile, Captain Styx, ever enigmatic and seemingly unfazed by the weight of their circumstances, strolled along with a carefree demeanor. His arms rested casually atop his head, and a nonchalant whistle escaped his lips. It was as if he held a secret understanding of the island's mysteries, an assurance that their path would lead them to the truth they sought.

Amelia cast a glance at Captain Styx, her voice choked with emotion. "Captain, how can you be so calm? Carlos sacrificed himself for us, and now he's gone."

The captain turned his gaze towards Amelia, his eyes reflecting an ancient wisdom. "Amelia, my dear, I understand your grief. Carlos's sacrifice was noble, and we shall never forget him," he said, his voice gentle yet resolute. "But we must press on. We have a purpose here on Mirage Island, and dwelling solely on our sorrows will not lead us to the answers we seek."

Amelia nodded, wiping away her tears. She took a deep breath, determined to find the strength to carry on. "You're right, Captain. Carlos wouldn't want us to falter. We owe it to him to uncover the truth."

Milo, finding solace in Amelia's words, nodded in agreement. "We'll honor Carlos's memory by completing our mission," he said, his voice filled with a newfound determination.

As the sun began its descent, casting a warm golden glow upon the island, Captain Styx surveyed their surroundings. He turned to Amelia and Milo, his voice calm and measured, "It's time to set up camp for the night. We'll need our strength for the journey ahead."

Amelia nodded, wiping away the remnants of her tears, her gaze fixed on the fading horizon. "You're right, Captain. We should rest and gather our thoughts. We have a long way to go."

Milo, still grappling with the weight of their recent experiences, glanced around, searching for a suitable spot to settle.

I trio ventured further into the island's interior, in search of a safe haven for the night. As darkness gradually blanketed the land, they stumbled upon a small clearing nestled amidst the dense foliage. The moonlight filtered through the treetops, casting ethereal patterns upon the ground.

Captain Styx took the lead, his experienced hands deftly setting up a makeshift camp. Amelia and Milo assisted, their movements a dance of coordination and weariness. They worked in silence, the crackling of the fire and the rustling of leaves punctuating the stillness of the night.

With the camp set, Amelia and Milo gathered around the flickering flames, seeking warmth and solace. The weariness of their journey weighed upon their shoulders, their bodies longing for rest. But sleep seemed elusive, their minds still wrestling with the enigmas of Mirage Island.

Captain Styx, ever perceptive, observed their troubled expressions. He sat beside them, his voice a soothing balm in the darkness. "Rest, my friends. Let the mysteries of this island wait till tomorrow. We've come a long way, and we'll need our strength for what lies ahead."

Amelia sighed, leaning back against a tree, her eyes fixed on the dancing flames. "You're right, Captain. We should take this moment to gather our thoughts and find some respite."

Milo nodded in agreement, his gaze drifting towards the starry sky. "We'll need all the strength we can muster. Carlos sacrificed himself for us. We owe it to him to push forward."

The fire crackled and cast dancing shadows upon their faces as they sat in silence, the weight of their shared burdens intertwining with the calm of the night. They found solace in each other's presence, a silent support that bound them together amidst the uncertainties that surrounded them.

As the night deepened, their weariness began to outweigh their worries. They found comfort in the gentle lullaby of the island, the rustling of leaves and the distant murmur of waves. With heavy hearts and a glimmer of hope, they closed their eyes, surrendering to the embrace of sleep.

As Amelia opened her eyes, her surroundings shifted dramatically. Instead of the campfire and the familiar sounds of the island, she found herself standing in the midst of a serene body of water. No horizon was in sight, creating an otherworldly and disorienting atmosphere. Panic gripped her heart as she searched for a sense of direction, her mind racing with questions.

But just as despair threatened to consume her, a voice called out from behind, breaking through the stillness. Startled, Amelia turned swiftly, her eyes widening in astonishment and joy. Standing there, a few steps away, was Carlos. His familiar smile adorned his face, and his presence filled her with a mixture of relief and disbelief.

"Carlos!" Amelia exclaimed, her voice a mixture of surprise and delight. She rushed towards him, her feet gliding effortlessly through the calm waters, their touch cool and comforting against her skin. As she reached his side, she couldn't help but wrap her arms around him in a tight embrace, as if trying to ensure that he was truly there.

Carlos returned her embrace, his arms encircling her with warmth and reassurance. "Amelia," he whispered, his voice filled with affection and relief. "I'm here. I promised I wouldn't leave you again."

Amelia's eyes brimmed with tears of joy and relief as she pulled back slightly to look into his eyes. The once hauntingly familiar void that had accompanied her was replaced by the comfort of Carlos's presence. She found solace in his gaze, a reaffirmation of their unbreakable bond.

Carlos took a deep breath, his eyes filled with a mixture of sorrow and determination as he began to explain the deal he had made with the otherworldly being. Amelia's brow furrowed, struggling to comprehend the weight of his words, but Carlos reassured her with a gentle touch.

"It's okay, Amelia," he said, his voice soothing and filled with a sense of resolve. "I made a deal to protect you, and to ensure everyone's safety, but it comes at a cost. You have to reach the temple at the center of Mirage Island."

Amelia's eyes widened with a mixture of surprise and concern. "I... what does that mean?" she asked, her voice tinged with worry.

Carlos took her hand in his, intertwining their fingers as he looked deeply into her eyes. "The being that saved everyone only did it as long as I promised eternal servitude to it. But there's a way for me to come back to break the deal, but I'll need your help."

Amelia's heart ached with conflicting emotions, torn between the desperation to be fully reunited with Carlos and the lingering sense of uncertainty. Yet, she found solace in his touch, in the unwavering commitment he showed. She knew that whatever lay ahead, they would face it together.

"We'll find a way, Carlos," Amelia whispered, her voice filled with determination. "We'll reach that temple, and we'll make it through this. I believe in us."

Carlos nodded, a small smile tugging at the corners of his lips. "I believe in us too, Amelia. You've come this far, and you won't give up now. Together, we'll face whatever challenges await us and find a way to break the deal I made and be together once again."

Amelia's arms wrapped tightly around Carlos, clinging to him as if trying to hold onto every precious moment. Tears streamed down her face as she whispered, "I don't want you to go, Carlos. I can't bear the thought of losing you again."

Carlos held her gently, his embrace filled with both love and sadness. "I know, Amelia," he murmured softly. "But it's time for me to go. Open your eyes."

Reluctantly, Amelia obeyed his words, her tear-stained gaze meeting the morning light. As she opened her eyes, she found herself lying by the tree next to the campsite on Mirage Island once more, the rising sun casting a warm golden glow upon the land.

Amelia's heart skipped a beat, a mix of confusion and hope flooding her senses. "Carlos?" she called out tentatively, searching for any sign of his presence.

Amelia's eyes held a lingering sadness as she looked into the concerned gazes of Captain Styx and Milo. Their unspoken worry hung in the air, mingling with the morning breeze. The captain's deep voice cut through the silence, breaking the fragile moment.

"Amelia, are you all right?" he inquired, his tone revealing his genuine concern.

Amelia forced a smile, her voice wavering slightly as she replied, "I'm fine, Captain. Just lost in thought, that's all."

Milo exchanged a worried glance with the captain, but they respected Amelia's desire to keep her emotions to herself. The weight of her dream and the bittersweet encounter with Carlos lingered within her, yet she knew it was something she needed to process on her own.

The captain grunted, his rugged face etched with a mix of understanding and determination. "We don't have much time to dwell on our emotions, my dear," he declared, his voice firm. "It's time to press on, continue our journey."

Amelia nodded, gathering her strength and resolve. She took a deep breath, pushing the melancholy thoughts to the back of her mind. The island's mysteries awaited them, and they had a mission to fulfill.

As they continued their trek through the dense foliage, Milo couldn't help but notice the unusual quietness that had settled upon Amelia. Concern etched his features as he glanced at her, his voice laced with gentle curiosity.

"Amelia, you've been awfully quiet. Is everything all right?" he asked, his concern evident in his tone.

Amelia's gaze shifted momentarily, her lips curving into a half-hearted smile. "Oh, I'm just lost in my thoughts, Milo," she replied, her voice tinged with a touch of evasiveness.

Milo sensed that there was more to her silence than she was letting on, but he respected her need for privacy. He couldn't help but wonder what troubled her, but he also understood that everyone had their own way of dealing with emotions.

Walking a few steps ahead of them, Captain Styx glanced back briefly, his sharp eyes narrowing ever so slightly as he observed Amelia's guarded demeanor. He recognized the hesitation in her voice, the hidden burden that she carried. Yet, he chose to leave it untouched for now, respecting her right to keep her thoughts to herself.

The captain's steps quickened, his powerful presence leading the way through the winding paths of the island. Amelia and Milo followed suit, their footsteps blending with the rustle of leaves and the distant songs of birds.

Amelia couldn't shake off the sensation of being enveloped in a veil of secrecy. The memory of her dream, the encounter with Carlos, still lingered in her mind, its weight growing heavier with each passing moment. Yet, she remained determined to keep it locked away, unsure of how it would be received.

The trio had been making steady progress through the dense foliage when Captain Styx abruptly halted, his senses alert to an unseen presence. Amelia's voice broke the silence, her concern evident as she inquired about the captain's sudden stop.

"Why did you stop, Captain?" she asked, her voice tinged with a mixture of curiosity and apprehension.

Captain Styx turned slightly, his gaze piercing through the shadows as he spoke with a sense of urgency. "We're being followed," he replied, his voice low and filled with a hint of caution.

Amelia's eyes widened, her heart quickening its pace as the weight of their predicament settled upon her. Milo shifted uneasily, his body tensing in anticipation of the unknown threat that lurked behind them.

The captain's instincts rarely led him astray, and the gravity of his words resonated within the trio's collective consciousness. They knew that the enigmatic nature of the island brought with it both wonders and perils, and it seemed they had unwittingly drawn the attention of a lurking danger.

The air grew heavy with an eerie stillness as the sound of twigs snapping in the bushes pierced the silence. The trio turned their heads in unison, their eyes widening in alarm as two lanky figures emerged from the shadows. These beings, clad in tattered garments, moved with an unsettling gait, their forms distorted and twisted. Their mouths were sewn shut, preventing any sound from escaping, and an inky blackness seemed to emanate from their very beings.

Amelia's heart skipped a beat, her breath catching in her throat at the sight of these otherworldly figures. She instinctively moved closer to the captain, seeking solace and protection in his presence. Milo's grip on a large stick he found nearby tightened, ready to defend himself and his companions against this unknown threat.

"What... What are they?" Amelia stammered, her voice barely a whisper, her eyes fixated on the grotesque figures before them.

The captain's expression hardened, his eyes narrowing as he assessed the looming danger. "I've encountered beings like this before," he replied, his voice filled with a mix of caution and determination. "They are not to be underestimated."

Milo's knuckles turned white as he tightened his grip on his weapon, his voice determined as he spoke. "We can't let them get any closer!"

The figures moved closer, their unnerving presence sending shivers down the trio's spines. The inky darkness seemed to pulsate within them, as if they were vessels of an ancient, malevolent force.

As the two figures drew closer, an unnerving transformation overcame them. Their bodies contorted and twisted, their limbs elongating and shifting in a grotesque display of otherworldly power. The inky blackness that surrounded them swirled and writhed, as if it were alive and feeding on their newfound monstrous forms.

Amelia's eyes widened in horror, her voice trembling as she uttered, "What are they becoming? This can't be real!"

The grotesque figures completed their transformation, their forms now a twisted amalgamation of horrifying features. One took on the shape of a gnarled, deformed beast, with sharp fangs, claws like razors, and a hulking, misshapen body. The other morphed into a shadowy apparition, oozing darkness and despair, its eyes glowing with an ethereal malevolence.

The air crackled with an electric intensity as the monstrous creatures loomed before the trio. The very fabric of reality seemed to warp and contort in their presence. Fear threatened to grip Amelia and Milo's heart, but they forced themselves to stand tall, Milo readying his weapon.

Amidst the chaos and the looming threat of the grotesque

creatures, Amelia's voice quivered with desperation as she whispered, "What do we do now?"

Captain Styx slowly leaned turned Amelia and whispered one word to her, "Run."

Without a moment's hesitation, the trio spun around, their hearts pounding in their chests as they sprinted away from the abominations that pursued them. The captain's voice rang out, guiding them through the labyrinthine paths of the island.

"Run! Head to the center of the island. It's our only chance of survival!"

"Keep moving! Stay together!" he bellowed, his voice laced with a mixture of determination and concern.

Amidst their desperate race towards the center of the island, a sudden cry of distress pierced through the air as Milo lost his footing, tumbling down a treacherous slope. Panic surged through Amelia's veins as she witnessed the horrifying sight. She called out to Milo, her voice filled with fear and urgency. "Milo! Hold on!"

The Captain's eyes widened, his face etched with concern, but he knew they couldn't afford to lose momentum. "Amelia, we have to keep going! We can't let them catch up!"

Reluctantly, Amelia tore her gaze away from Milo's perilous situation, her heart heavy with worry. She took a deep breath, forcing herself to focus on their shared goal. "You're right, Captain. We have to keep moving."

They pressed on, their footsteps quickening as they left Milo behind, their determination to reach the island's center burning brighter than ever. The monstrous creatures, undeterred by Milo's fall, relentlessly pursued the trio, their dark forms bounding over the terrain with unnerving agility.

Amelia stole a glance over her shoulder, her voice quivering with concern. "What about Milo, Captain? We can't just leave him behind!"

The captain's voice carried a mix of regret and determination. "I know it's hard, Amelia, but our best chance is to keep going. We can't let these creatures consume us too."

As they pushed forward, the ground beneath them grew uneven, the island's treacherous terrain threatening to impede their progress. The captain skillfully maneuvered through the obstacles, leading the way with unwavering resolve. Amelia followed closely behind, her eyes scanning the surroundings, ready to face any new threat that may arise.

The monsters, closing in on them, let out ear-piercing screeches that reverberated through the air. Their distorted forms seemed to contort with each movement, their grotesque features horrifying to behold. But the captain's voice carried a resolute tone, urging Amelia to keep going. "Don't look back, Amelia! Focus on what's ahead!"

With each passing moment, the distance between them and the center of the island diminished, hope flickering within their hearts. The captain's voice resonated with unwavering determination. "Just a little farther! We're almost there!"

Amelia's breaths came in ragged gasps as she matched the captain's pace, her legs burning with exertion. Though the weight of Milo's absence tugged at her heart, she clung to the belief that they were forging a path to safety, and perhaps, a chance to rescue their fallen friend.

As the adrenaline-fueled sprint brought them closer to the center of the island, Captain Styx's eyes widened with a mix of relief and anticipation. "There it is, Amelia! The temple! Our sanctuary!"

With the monstrous creature closing in on them, the captain and Amelia pushed their bodies to the limit, leaping through the temple doorway just in time. As they tumbled onto the cold stone floor, their chests heaving with exhaustion, they turned their gaze back to the entrance, their hearts pounding in their chests.

The monstrous figure, unaware of the invisible barrier that shielded the temple, charged forward with unyielding determination. But as it reached the threshold, its momentum abruptly halted, as if colliding with an impenetrable force. The creature let out a guttural shriek, its pain echoing through the air, before stumbling backward, its balance disrupted by the unseen resistance.

Amelia and the captain exchanged wide-eyed glances, their bodies trembling from both exertion and the relief of sanctuary. Gasping for breath, Amelia managed to utter a few words, her voice laced with a mix of astonishment and gratitude. "Captain... we made it. We're safe."

The captain nodded, his voice slightly strained but filled with satisfaction. "Yes, Amelia. For now, we are safe within these ancient walls. But we must remain vigilant. This temple holds its own secrets, and we have yet to uncover its purpose."

Amelia's voice trembled with urgency as she shouted, "We need to save Milo! We can't just leave him out there!"

The captain, his face etched with a mixture of concern and determination, gently but firmly grabbed Amelia's arm, halting her in her tracks. He pointed towards the entrance, where the monstrous creature paced back and forth, its monstrous form casting an ominous shadow across the temple floor.

"We have no choice, Amelia," the captain said, his voice filled with both resignation and caution. "Look at that creature. It guards the entrance, barring our escape. There's no way for us to leave and help Milo. We must stay here and hope that he can find his own way to the temple."

Amelia's heart sank, a mixture of fear and frustration coursing through her veins. She clenched her fists, her eyes darting between the captain and the entrance, torn between the instinct to protect her friend and the logic of the captain's words.

"But... what if Milo can't make it? What if he's captured or worse?" Amelia's voice wavered, her voice filled with anguish and desperation.

The captain's grip on her arm tightened, his gaze unwavering. "We must trust in Milo's strength and resourcefulness. He is capable, Amelia. He has proven it before. We have to believe that he will find a way to reach us."

Amelia bit her lip, her eyes still fixed on the entrance where the creature continued its relentless patrol. Tears welled up in her eyes, her voice barely above a whisper. "I just hope he's okay... that he's still alive."

The captain's voice softened as he placed a hand on Amelia's shoulder, offering a reassuring squeeze. "We all hope for the same, Amelia. We must remain hopeful and united. Milo is a survivor, and we will not abandon him. But for now, we can only wait here and be ready for his arrival. We have to believe in his strength and resilience."

Amelia nodded, her eyes filled with a mix of determination and worry. As they settled into their temporary refuge within the temple, Amelia's thoughts were consumed by Milo, hoping that he would find his way through the treacherous island and reunite with them.

Milo's eyes fluttered open, his head throbbing with pain. Groaning, he struggled to sit up, his body protesting every movement. As his vision cleared, he took in the grim reality before him—a deep ravine, its walls towering above him like a prison. He attempted to stand, but his legs gave way, sending waves of agony through his body.

Just as despair began to grip Milo's heart, a guttural growl pierced the silence, causing him to freeze. His gaze shifted upwards, and a jolt of terror shot through his veins. There, perched on the edge of the ravine, was the monstrous creature, its monstrous form silhouetted against the dim light above.

Milo's heart raced, his breath catching in his throat. His mind raced with fear and uncertainty, his body feeling weak and vulnerable. The creature's eyes locked onto him, its growl growing louder as it started to crawl down the ravine, its movements grotesque and unnatural.

Panic surged through Milo's veins as he scrambled to find a way to escape. He gritted his teeth against the pain, determination fueling his actions. With a surge of adrenaline, he crawled toward a nearby crevice, using all his strength to pull himself forward. Each movement sent waves of agony coursing through his battered body, but he pushed through, driven by sheer willpower.

As the creature drew nearer, its hungry gaze fixed upon Milo, he could feel its malevolent presence, a chilling reminder of the danger that awaited him. With a burst of desperation, Milo mustered the last reserves of his strength and managed to crawl into the narrow crevice, his body wedged tightly between the unforgiving walls.

The creature let out a frustrated roar, its claws scraping against the rock, unable to reach its prey. Milo's heart pounded in his chest, his breath coming in short gasps. He knew he was not safe yet, but for the moment, he was out of the creature's immediate reach.

Grimacing in pain, Milo closed his eyes briefly, his mind racing for a plan. He knew he had to find a way out of the ravine and make his way back to his friends.

Milo's gaze shifted from the creature looming at the mouth of the crevice to the dark, narrow passage stretching before him. The realization dawned upon him that he couldn't retreat the way he had come. The creature's piercing eyes fixed upon him, a constant reminder of the danger lurking just outside.

Taking a deep breath, Milo steeled himself and made a decision. He knew that venturing deeper into the crevice carried its own risks, but it seemed to be his only chance for escape. With a mix of trepidation and hope, he began to inch forward, the walls of the crevice closing in around him._

Chapter Sixteen
A NARROW ESCAPE

Milo's weary body had reached its limit, unable to bear the strain any longer. With each step he took, his strength waned, and finally, his legs gave way beneath him. He collapsed onto the cold, stone floor of the crevice, his body trembling with exhaustion and pain.

Through gritted teeth, he muttered, "I... I can't go on... anymore." His voice was barely a whisper, a reflection of his dwindling spirit. The crevice seemed to taunt him, its walls closing in, suffocating him with their oppressive presence.

He closed his eyes, ready to succumb to exhaustion and pain. But just as his consciousness began to fade, a faint glow of soft blue emanated from the depths of the crevice, gently caressing his weary form.

A delicate voice, barely audible, echoed in Milo's ears, stirring his fading awareness. "Milo... Don't give up. Your friends need you," the voice whispered, carrying a mix of urgency and compassion. The words penetrated his soul, reigniting a spark of determination within him.

With a surge of willpower, Milo pushed himself up, wincing at the renewed wave of pain coursing through his body. The blue light grew brighter, guiding his way forward. Step by excruciating step, he persevered, following the ethereal glow deeper into the crevice.

Back at the temple, Amelia's anxiety grew with each passing moment, her eyes darting back and forth in search of any sign of Milo. Hours had slipped away, yet there was no trace of him. Frustration mixed with worry, threatening to overpower her resolve.

Seeing Amelia's distress, Captain Styx approached her cautiously, his voice laced with concern. "Amelia, I understand your fear and frustration, but if we don't keep moving forward, all that we've endured, all the sacrifices made, will be in vain," he gently reasoned.

Amelia's eyes welled up with tears as she turned to face the captain. Her voice quivered with a mix of anger and sadness. "But Captain, Milo is out there. We can't just leave him behind," she pleaded, her hands trembling with emotion.

The captain's gaze softened, his tone filled with empathy. "I know, Amelia. Believe me, it pains me as well. But we have a responsibility to honor Milo's sacrifice and continue our mission. We must continue."

Amelia's frustration clashed with the captain's reasoning. Her heart wavered between wanting to stay and wait for Milo and understanding the necessity of their mission. The weight of the captain's words settled upon her, resonating with the truth they held.

Tears streamed down Amelia's cheeks as she took a deep breath, attempting to regain her composure. She looked into the captain's eyes, her voice now resolute but tinged with sadness. "Okay, Captain. Let's keep moving forward," she reluctantly agreed, the weight of her decision settling upon her shoulders.

With a heavy heart, Amelia wiped away her tears and steeled herself for the arduous journey ahead. The captain nodded in appreciation, his eyes filled with a mixture of sorrow and determination. Together, they pushed forward.

As Captain Styx and Amelia ventured further into the temple, their eyes were drawn to the intricate details etched into the walls. The soft glow of torchlight danced upon the ancient carvings, casting shadows that seemed to come alive with each step.

Amelia's unknowingly held her breath as she beheld a mesmerizing mural depicting a great battle. Celestial beings clashed against a backdrop of swirling galaxies, their forms frozen in eternal struggle. Each stroke of the artist's hand brought forth a sense of grandeur and power, capturing the cosmic forces at play.

"Captain, look at this!" Amelia exclaimed, her voice filled with awe. "It's as if the very heavens are at war. The artistry is beyond breathtaking."

The captain turned his gaze to the mural, his eyes widening in astonishment. "Truly magnificent," he murmured, his voice filled with reverence. "It seems to tell a story of celestial forces locked in an eternal battle for supremacy."

Amelia nodded in agreement, her eyes tracing the intricate details of the mural. The celestial beings seemed to dance across the walls, their expressions conveying both determination and anguish. She couldn't help but feel a sense of wonder to the cosmic drama unfolding before her.

Distracted by the mural, Amelia was oblivious to her surroundings. Amelia's foot unknowingly pressed upon a concealed pressure plate; a low rumble echoed through the chamber. In an instant, the floor beneath her gave way, revealing a hidden slope leading into an abyss of darkness. Terror seized her heart, and a piercing scream escaped her lips as she plummeted into the unknown.

"Amelia!" Captain Styx shouted, his voice laced with urgency and desperation. He lunged forward, stretching out his arm in a desperate attempt to grab hold of her. His fingers brushed against her outstretched hand, but before he could secure his grip, Amelia slipped through his grasp, vanishing into the unfathomable depths below.

Time seemed to stand still as the captain stared into the void, his heart pounding in his chest. The echoes of Amelia's screams faded into silence, leaving behind a hollow emptiness. The captain's eyes widened in disbelief and anguish as he grappled with the realization that his companion had been snatched away in an instant.

"No... Amelia!" he whispered, his voice trembling with sorrow and regret. He could still hear the echoes of her screams reverberating in his ears, haunting reminders of the tragedy that had unfolded before him.

Amelia, hold on! I'm coming for you!" Captain Styx's voice echoed through the darkness, filled with determination and concern. His eyes darted around, searching for any sign of a way to reach his fallen companion.

Just as he was about to slide down the treacherous slope,

an unsettling whisper reached his ears, causing the hairs to stand on the back of his neck. The captain's eyes widened, his heart pounding in his chest. "Who's there?" he called out, his voice trembling.

Silence lingered for a moment, and then the eerie voice whispered his name once more, a faint echo that seemed to come from all directions. The captain's brow furrowed, his mind racing with questions. Despite his apprehension, a flicker of curiosity ignited within him, compelling him to seek out the source of the mysterious whisperer.

Slowly, cautiously, he followed the ethereal voice, his footsteps echoing through the chamber. Shadows danced along the walls, casting eerie shapes that seemed to taunt him. The air grew colder, thick with an otherworldly presence. As he ventured deeper into the unknown, a mix of trepidation and determination filled his being.

With each step, the captain's resolve wavered between caution and the need to uncover the truth. The voice called to him, its whispers beckoning him forward like a siren's song. His heart thudded in his chest as he navigated the labyrinthine corridors, his senses on high alert.

The captain cautiously stepped into a chamber, his eyes quickly fixed on a figure standing in the far corner. It appeared as a spectral entity, its form ethereal and translucent, as if it were made of mist and moonlight.

The captain's footsteps echoed through the chamber as he cautiously approached the spectral figure in the far corner. His voice trembled as he spoke. "Who are you?" The room seemed to grow colder, and a faint crying sound reached his ears, tugging at his heart.

As he drew nearer, the figure slowly turned around, revealing its ghostly form. The captain's breath caught in his throat, and his legs weakened beneath him, causing him to fall to his knees. Before him stood a haunting vision of his past, a spectral manifestation that stirred deep emotions within him.

Tears streamed down the captain's face as he gazed upon the figure, his voice choked with a mix of sorrow and disbelief. "It can't be... Is it truly you?" The ghostly form nodded, its eyes filled with a mixture of sadness and longing.

The figure, bathed in an otherworldly glow, reached out a translucent hand towards the captain's outstretched arm. As their fingertips brushed, the light intensified, revealing deep cuts etched along the figure's wrist—a painful reminder of a tragic end.

Tears welled up in the captain's eyes as he traced the scars with trembling fingers, his voice filled with anguish. "I failed you...." The spectral figure, a bittersweet embodiment of love and loss, remained silent.

As the specter aggressively pulled her arm away from the captain's grasp, its ethereal form seemed to grow more tangible, emanating an air of anger and accusation. Its voice, once soft and melancholic, now boomed with an unsettling intensity.

"It is all your fault!" the specter declared, its spectral voice reverberating through the chamber. "If you would have listened to me, none of this would have happened!" The words struck the captain like a piercing arrow, his heart heavy with guilt and remorse.

The captain's eyes filled with tears as he desperately pleaded for forgiveness. "I'm sorry," he cried, his voice filled with anguish. "I tried... I didn't notice in time. Please, I'm sorry."

The specter turned from the captain, fleeing towards a wall, its wails echoing throughout the chamber. As it reached the wall, it glided on through, leaving behind a plume of dust.

As the specter's form dissolved into dust, the captain remained knelt on the ground, his heart heavy with grief. The chamber grew silent, save for the soft echoes of his sobs. In the stillness, a haunting whisper seemed to brush against his ear, repeating the words that weighed heavily on his conscience.

"It was all your fault."

The captain's breath caught in his throat as he turned his head, searching for the source of the voice. But the chamber offered no solace, only the remnants of the specter's presence and the lingering echoes of his past mistakes.

Tears streamed down the captain's face as he struggled to come to terms with the truth of those words. The weight of his guilt threatened to consume him, an agonizing reminder of the choices he had made and the consequences they had brought upon his loved ones.

As the captain knelt on the chamber floor, consumed by grief, a faint voice reached his ears. He turned his head, startled by the sound of a small child's voice, uttering a single word that held immense significance.

"Papa."

The captain could not breathe as he slowly turned around, his eyes widening in disbelief. There, standing behind him, was a young boy, his eyes shimmering with innocence and love. His heart skipped a beat as he recognized him as his own son, a child he had believed he had lost forever.

The captain, his heart bursting with remorse and longing, crawled towards the spectral child and enveloped him in a desperate, tearful embrace. His voice cracked with emotion as he offered his sincerest apologies, repeating them over and over again, as if trying to wash away the pain he had caused.

"I'm so sorry... I failed you... Please forgive me," the captain pleaded, his voice choked with sorrow. He held the child tightly, desperately seeking some form of solace in this fragile reunion.

But the spectral child remained silent, his ethereal form seemingly unmoved by the captain's words. His translucent figure radiated an aura of melancholy, a haunting reminder of the sorrow and regret that haunted the captain's soul.

The captain clung to the child, burying his face in the ghostly wisps of his son's hair, unwilling to let go. His tears mingled with the spectral essence, a poignant blend of grief and longing.

The captain froze, his heart pounding in his chest as the spectral child's voice cut through the air like a chilling wind. The child's words echoed with accusation and pain, seeping into the captain's very core.

"Why did you do this to me?" the spectral child repeated, his voice haunting and filled with anguish. The captain's hands trembled as he slowly turned to face the child, his eyes widening in terror.

But as he looked into the child's face, a horrifying realization struck him. The child's once-vibrant eyes were now hollow sockets, devoid of life and filled with darkness.

Fear gripped the captain's heart, and he instinctively pushed the specter away, recoiling from its unnatural presence. The once-familiar form of his child seemed to contort and distort.

The captain's heart raced as he scrambled backward, his eyes fixed on the approaching specter. The specter, with its hollow eyes and distorted form, continued its relentless advance, its voice growing more eerie and distorted with each repetition of its haunting question.

"Why did you do this to me?" the specter repeated, its words slurred and muffled, as if spoken underwater. The captain could feel the weight of its accusation pressing down upon him, its relentless pursuit intensifying his fear and guilt.

The spectral figure moved methodically, each step echoing through the chamber with an otherworldly resonance. Its distorted voice filled the air, creating an unsettling atmosphere that sent shivers down the captain's spine.

The specter's steps transformed into a peculiar sloshing sound, reminiscent of water being forcefully moved. The specter's distorted voice, filled with accusation and torment, gave way to a gurgling, as if it was struggling to breathe beneath the depths of an unseen ocean.

Incredibly, the specter continued its relentless approach, its form shifting and swirling, as if composed of liquid darkness. The captain braced himself, uncertainty gripping his every fiber.

But just as the specter loomed within a few feet of the captain, its watery essence surged forward, splashing down at his feet. The gurgling voice dissipated, replaced by the gentle sound of water cascading onto the chamber floor.

The captain remained frozen in place, his body trembling with fear as tears streamed down his weathered face. The weight of the encounter with the specter and its haunting words had taken a toll on his spirit. His mind raced, grappling with a flood of emotions and questions that seemed to have no answers.

As the captain sat in the chamber, still unable to move, consumed by his own inner turmoil, a wispy form began to seep into the room, materializing like swirling smoke. The figure took the shape of the Messenger, its presence ethereal and haunting. Its voice echoed in the captain's mind, filling his thoughts with a chilling whisper.

"You failed them," the voice hissed, its words intertwining with the captain's thoughts. "Your wife, your son... Their deaths were on your hands."

Visions flooded the captain's mind, vivid and agonizing. He saw himself clutching his son, his small, lifeless body drenched in water, the vision changed to him kneeling beside his wife lying motionless in a blood-soaked dress.

"And now," the spectral Messenger continued, its voice a chilling whisper, "you will fail Amelia and Milo as well. Their deaths will be a consequence of your actions."

Visions once again flickered before the captain's eyes, grotesque and harrowing. He saw himself cradling the lifeless bodies of Amelia and Milo, their pale forms limp and broken. The weight of those imaginary losses pressed upon his chest, suffocating him with guilt and dread.

"No," the captain protested, his voice strained but determined. "I won't let that happen. I won't allow their lives to be taken from me. I will protect them."

But the Messenger's whispers persisted, infiltrating the captain's thoughts with doubt and despair. It twisted the knife deeper into his wounds, exploiting his deepest fears and insecurities.

"You cannot protect anyone," the Messenger taunted, its voice growing louder and more malicious. "You are destined to bring only death and sorrow."

As the captain's determination blazed within him, the wispy Messenger surged forward, its ethereal form solidifying into a ghastly figure. With an eerie strength, it seized the captain by the sides of his head, lifting him effortlessly into the air. The captain fought with all his might, struggling against the vice-like grip, but his efforts seemed feeble in the face of the Messenger's malevolence.

"Let go!" the captain growled, his voice a mix of defiance and desperation. He squirmed and writhed, his muscles straining against the unyielding hold, but the Messenger only chuckled darkly, relishing in the captain's struggle.

"Oh, dear captain," the messenger sneered, its voice dripping with sinister delight. "Do you truly believe you can escape your fate? Your resistance is amusing, but ultimately futile."

As the captain hung there, his victorious resolve still pulsating within him, a sinister cloud of black smoke billowed forth. It snaked its way towards him, its tendrils curling and contorting with an ominous intent. Before the captain could react, the malevolent entity forced its way into his open mouth, infiltrating his very being.

Agony washed over the captain as the smoke penetrated every fiber of his being. He convulsed, his body wracked with pain, while tears streamed down his anguished face. The burning sensation intensified, coursing through his veins like liquid fire. His clenched fists trembled uncontrollably as he tried to endure the excruciating torment.

The Messenger's laughter echoed in the air, a wicked symphony of derision. "Delicious," it hissed, relishing in the captain's suffering. "Your pain fuels me, Captain. I shall revel in the chaos that ensues."

As the captain's body crashed to the cold, stone floor, a thunderous thud reverberated through the chamber. His convulsions continued, erratic and spasmodic, while the air grew heavy with an unsettling aura. All seemed lost as the captain lay motionless, his once-piercing gaze extinguished.

But then, with an otherworldly energy, the captain's eyes snapped open. What once held wisdom and vitality now brimmed with an inky blackness, void of any semblance of humanity.

A sinister smile stretched across the captain's face, a sinister grin that seemed to hold secrets and malevolence. It curled at the corners, revealing teeth that glinted with an unholy luster.

In a voice that dripped with maleficence, the captain spoke, his words laced with a dark allure. "Ah, this is going to be fun."_

Chapter Seventeen
THE ROOM OF MIRRORS

Amelia's eyelids fluttered, fighting against the weight of exhaustion. With each labored breath, she coughed, sending a cloud of dust swirling through the air. Blinking away the grit, she struggled to her feet, wincing as pain shot through her body.

As her vision cleared, she surveyed her surroundings. She stood in the center of a chamber, its walls adorned with mirrors from floor to ceiling. Each reflective surface seemed to hold a story of its own, reflecting her disheveled appearance back at her. A sense of unease crept over her, a feeling of being watched by unseen eyes.

"Captain!" Amelia's voice echoed through the chamber, desperation lacing every syllable. Her plea reverberated off the mirror-lined walls, but there was no response, only an eerie silence that enveloped her.

Tears welled in Amelia's eyes as she pressed her hand against one of the mirrors, hoping to find solace within its surface. The mirror felt icy cold against her skin, and a shiver ran down her spine. Fear gripped her heart as she realized she was trapped, surrounded by the enigmatic mirrors with no sign of the captain's presence.

"Captain, where are you?" she whispered, her voice barely audible, as if swallowed by the mysterious chamber. But there was no response, no reassuring voice to guide her. She was alone.

Amelia's eyes darted from mirror to mirror, her frantic gaze searching for any sign of an exit. But no matter how hard she looked, there was no visible escape route from the confining chamber. The mirrors seemed to mock her, reflecting back her anxious face in countless distorted angles.

Panic gripped Amelia's chest as she pressed her hands against the smooth surface of one mirror after another, desperately hoping to find a hidden latch or a concealed door. But her efforts proved futile, as the mirrors remained steadfast, offering no passage to freedom.

"Where is the way out?" Amelia's voice trembled with frustration and desperation, her words echoing through the chamber. But there was no answer, only the haunting silence that hung in the air, suffocating her hopes.

Her breaths came in shallow gasps as she continued to scan the room, her eyes widening with each passing moment. The mirrored walls seemed to close in on her, their reflections distorting her perception of space and time. She felt trapped, ensnared in a labyrinthine puzzle with no solution in sight.

Amelia stood in the midst of the mirrored chamber, her mind racing as she desperately tried to come up with a plan. Frustration and fear gnawed at her, but she knew she couldn't afford to succumb to panic. With her hands pressed firmly against her closed eyes, she tried to shut out the disorienting reflections surrounding her.

"Think, Amelia, think," she whispered to herself, her voice tinged with a mix of determination and anxiety. She needed to find a solution, a way to navigate through the perplexing labyrinth of mirrors. But the answers eluded her, the darkness behind her eyelids offering no immediate respite.

Amelia's heart jumped as she heard her name whispered through the chamber. She blinked, scanning her surroundings, her eyes darting from one mirror to another, searching for the source of the ethereal voice. "Who's there?" she called out, her voice quivering with curiosity. Silence greeted her, and for a moment, she wondered if her mind was indeed playing tricks on her.

But then, the voice spoke again, this time from a different corner of the room. It seemed to dance on the edge of her hearing, teasing and elusive. "Amelia," it whispered, its tone both familiar and haunting. She strained her ears, trying to discern any clues about its origin, but the voice seemed to defy logic, appearing and disappearing like a ghostly presence.

Tentatively, Amelia stepped closer to one of the mirrors, her eyes locked on her own reflection. "Who are you?" she asked, her voice laced with a mix of anticipation and apprehension. Yet, once again, no immediate response came. The voice seemed to taunt her, dancing on the edge of her perception, always just out of reach.

Amelia's frustration and desperation reached a boiling point, and without thinking, she struck the mirror with her clenched fist. The impact reverberated through the chamber, causing cracks to spiderweb across the reflective surface. But instead of shattering, the mirror remained intact, taunting her with its unyielding barrier.

As Amelia turned around, her eyes widened in disbelief. Standing before her, Carlos, his image reflected in the mirror. Her heart raced, a whirlwind of emotions coursing through her veins. "Carlos?" she called out, her voice a mix of astonishment and longing.

Carlos smiled, his reflection mirroring the warmth in his eyes. "Amelia," he whispered, his voice resonating with a haunting familiarity. She took a step towards him, her heart yearning for his embrace. But as she reached out to touch him, her outstretched hand collided with the solid surface of the mirror, causing her to stumble backward and crash onto the cold, unforgiving ground.

Pain shot through Amelia's body as she lay there, her mind reeling from the shock of the collision. Tears welled up in her eyes as she gazed at the unattainable reflection of Carlos. "No," she cried, her voice filled with anguish. "Why can't I reach you?"

Carlos, his spectral form shimmering in the mirror, reached out to Amelia with a reassuring smile. "Amelia, the mirror is but a barrier, and barriers can be broken. The power to shatter it lies within this ancient temple itself."

Amelia, her eyes filled with both anticipation and uncertainty, asked, "How do we break it, Carlos?"

Carlos, his voice steady and resolute, explained, "The temple holds ancient powers that flow through its very walls. To break the barrier, we must harness that power, using it against itself." He nodded towards a seemingly ordinary stone lying on the ground, its unassuming presence contrasting with the grandeur of the temple. "The key lies within that stone, Amelia."

Amelia reached down and picked up the stone, feeling its weight in her palm. She could sense a faint energy emanating from it, as if it held a hidden power waiting to be unleashed. Gathering her strength, she clenched her fist around the stone, determination burning in her eyes.

With a surge of determination, Amelia summoned all her might and swung the stone at the mirror with all her force. The impact sent shockwaves rippling through the chamber, a thunderous crash reverberating through the air. The force of the impact threw Amelia backward, her body colliding with the ground.

As she struggled to regain her bearings, Amelia watched in awe as the mirror crumbled before her. Fragments of glass scattered across the chamber, revealing a hidden path that had been concealed behind the barrier. Light poured through the shattered remnants, casting intricate patterns on the chamber's walls.

Amelia stood amidst the shattered remnants of the barrier, her eyes scanning the chamber for any sign of Carlos. But to her dismay, he was nowhere to be found. She called out his name, her voice echoing through the empty space, but received no response.

Just as a pang of worry threatened to consume her, Amelia heard a faint whisper carried on a gentle breeze. "Amelia... follow me," the voice called, its ethereal quality both familiar and comforting.

Her heart pounding with anticipation, Amelia turned her attention to a hidden corridor that had been concealed behind the shattered mirror. It beckoned to her, its entrance veiled in shadows and mystery. With a mix of apprehension and determination, she took a step forward, drawn by the enigmatic allure of the whispered invitation.

As she ventured deeper into the hidden passage, a soft glow guided her way. The air grew cooler, and the faint scent of moss and ancient secrets enveloped her senses. With each step, the connection to Carlos seemed to grow stronger, his presence pulsating through the very fabric of the corridor.

"Carlos?" Amelia called out, her voice quivering with hope and anticipation. "Where are you?"

His whisper echoed around her, resonating in the depths of her being. "Trust your instincts, Amelia. Follow the path before you. I am here."

Amelia pressed on, guided by an invisible force, her footsteps steady and resolute. The corridor seemed to stretch endlessly, leading her deeper into the heart of the unknown. Shadows danced along the walls, casting eerie silhouettes that flickered with a life of their own.

The whisper grew louder, drawing her closer to its source. "Almost there, my love," Carlos's voice urged, the tenderness in his words echoing through the narrow passage. "Just a little farther."

Finally, the corridor opened up into a chamber bathed in a soft, radiant light. Amelia's eyes widened in awe as she beheld a mesmerizing sight—a hidden sanctuary, adorned with ancient symbols and mystical artifacts. And standing in the center of it all was Carlos standing next to a pedestal.

Carlos stood before Amelia, his figure bathed in a gentle glow that seemed to emanate from within. He gestured for her to come closer, a serene smile playing on his lips. Amelia's heart fluttered with excitement as she cautiously extended her arm towards him, her fingers trembling slightly.

"Carlos, is it really you?" she whispered, her voice laced with both hope and uncertainty.

Carlos nodded, his eyes shimmering with an otherworldly light. "Yes, Amelia. It's me," he replied, his voice filled with reassurance. "I've found a way to be here with you."

Her hesitation dissolved as she felt the warmth of his presence, the familiar energy that had always drawn her to him. With a leap of faith, Amelia closed the distance between them and wrapped her arms around Carlos in a tight embrace. She could feel the solidity of his form, his essence intertwined with hers.

Tears of relief and happiness streamed down Amelia's cheeks as she held onto him, not daring to let go. "I can't believe you're really here," she whispered, her voice quivering with emotion.

Carlos's embrace tightened, his touch conveying a sense of comfort and belonging. "I know it may seem unbelievable, Amelia, but our connection transcends the boundaries of this world," he said softly. "I made a pact to be with you, and here I stand, by your side."

Amelia marveled at the miracle before her, cherishing this precious moment. She knew deep within her heart that the bond they shared was stronger than any barrier, any doubt or fear. Together, they stood in that mystical chamber, a testament to the power of love and determination.

Amelia's curiosity piqued as she noticed the glass box atop the intricately adorned pedestal. She turned to Carlos, her eyes reflecting a mixture of wonder and intrigue. "What is that?" she asked, pointing towards the exquisite display.

Carlos smiled warmly, his gaze fixed upon the glass case. "Let me show you," he replied, his voice filled with a sense of anticipation. With a gentle touch, he reached out and carefully opened the glass box, revealing its hidden treasure.

Inside the box lay a breathtaking dagger, its hilt crafted from shimmering gold that seemed to radiate an ethereal glow. Amelia couldn't help but gasp at the sight, her eyes drawn to the intricate carvings adorning the side of the handle. There, delicately etched into the gold, was a meticulously crafted key.

Amelia's fingers twitched with a mixture of curiosity and reverence, as if the dagger was calling out to her. "What's it for?" she asked, her voice barely above a whisper.

Carlos looked at Amelia with a mixture of longing and sadness. He took a deep breath before speaking, his voice filled with a bittersweet tone. "Amelia, I need you to understand that I am not fully in your world," he began, his eyes searching hers for understanding.

Amelia's brows furrowed with concern as she listened intently to Carlos's words. She held her breath, waiting for him to continue.

"Breaking the mirror was just the first step," Carlos explained, his voice tinged with a hint of urgency. "To fully bridge the gap between our worlds, we need to complete one more task. It's the only way for us to be together, Amelia."

Amelia's heart sank. She wanted nothing more than to be by Carlos's side, to experience the love and adventure they had dreamed of. But she couldn't ignore the underlying uncertainty that hung in the air.

"What do I need to do, Carlos?" she asked, her voice filled with a blend of determination and vulnerability.

Carlos took Amelia's hands into his own, his touch reassuring and warm. "For now take the knife," he said, his voice filled with a sense of purpose. "Keep it hidden and reveal only when I tell you."

Amelia's heart fluttered with a mix of uncertainty and anticipation as she reluctantly agreed to Carlos's request. She couldn't shake off the feeling that there was so much she didn't know, so much she couldn't understand. But her love for Carlos propelled her forward, blinding her to the doubts that lingered in the depths of her mind.

Carlos's smile widened with a sense of relief and assurance. "Thank you, Amelia," he said, his voice filled with gratitude. "This is a path you must walk alone for now. But remember, I am with you always, even if you can't see me. Trust in our love, and it will guide you."

Amelia looked at the corridor Carlos was pointing to, a mixture of curiosity and apprehension filling her thoughts. "How long should I go down this path?" she asked, her voice tinged with uncertainty.

Carlos's expression turned serene, his eyes fixed on Amelia's. "You'll know when you get there," he replied cryptically. "The journey will reveal itself to you, and you'll find the answers you seek. Trust your instincts, Amelia, and follow your heart."

Amelia's footsteps echoed through the narrow corridor as she ventured further into the unknown. A mixture of determination and apprehension coursed through her veins, fueled by the absence of Carlos's presence. She couldn't help but look back, hoping to catch one last glimpse of him before she embarked on this solitary path.

But as her gaze swept over the chamber she had just left, it became painfully clear that Carlos was no longer there. A pang of sadness tugged at her heart, but she knew she had to press on. With a resolute sigh, she turned her back on the emptiness behind her and focused her gaze forward, determined to unravel the mysteries that lay ahead.

The corridor stretched out before her, bathed in a soft, ethereal glow that cast elongated shadows on the walls. Amelia's grip tightened around the golden-hilted dagger, drawing strength from its presence. She took a deep breath, steeling herself for the challenges that awaited her in this unknown realm._

Chapter Eighteen
THE THRONE ROOM

Amelia's footsteps echoed through the corridor, her journey stretching on for what felt like hours. Lost in her thoughts, her mind became a whirlwind of worries and concerns, eclipsing the passage of time. Images of Milo's safety danced in her mind, each step carrying her closer to the hope of his well-being.

Her thoughts also lingered on the captain, imagining him navigating the temple's intricate paths with a sense of purpose. She could almost hear his steady whistle, a comforting tune that echoed in her memory. It offered a glimmer of solace amidst the uncertainty that enveloped her.

But above all, Amelia couldn't escape her thoughts of Carlos. His presence lingered in her heart, an ethereal thread that connected them across realms. She replayed their moments together, the warmth of his smile, and the comfort of his words. Their bond, tested by the mysterious circumstances they found themselves in, fueled her determination to reunite with him.

As she walked, each step carried her deeper into the unknown, but her thoughts remained firmly anchored to her loved ones. Their well-being became the driving force behind her every move, lending her strength in moments of doubt.

Amelia's wearied steps echoed through the seemingly endless corridor, her mind fraught with questions about the length of this path. Doubts crept in, whispering uncertainties and testing her resolve. But just as her thoughts began to weigh heavily upon her, a glimmer of hope appeared in the distance. A room materialized, its presence beckoning her closer.

Remembering the perils of unawareness, Amelia drew upon her newfound caution. She restrained the impulse to sprint toward the room, recognizing that patience and vigilance were her allies in this perilous journey. She had learned the hard way that haste often led to unforeseen traps.

Amelia's steps grew slower as she approached the room ahead. An air of caution surrounded her, a lesson learned from her previous encounter with the treacherous room of mirrors. She couldn't afford to be reckless again.

She stood at the threshold of the room, her eyes widening in awe as she took in the breathtaking sight before her. The room seemed to radiate a sense of tranquility, as if it held a secret oasis amidst the chaos that surrounded them.

Her gaze was drawn upward, towards the celestial mural that adorned the ceiling. The intricate brushstrokes depicted serene beings traversing the heavens, their ethereal forms dancing across the celestial canvas. Amelia couldn't help but feel a sense of wonder and peace wash over her, momentarily easing the weight of her worries.

As her eyes wandered around the room, they settled upon a majestic throne, positioned on one side. It was a striking sight, crafted from an ancient tree that had witnessed the passage of time. Half of the tree still thrived, adorned with vibrant golden leaves and luscious golden fruit, while the other half appeared desolate, its branches bare and forgotten.

Amelia approached the throne, her fingers gently grazing the textured surface of the living and withered wood. She marveled at the stark contrast between the two halves, symbolizing the duality of life itself. It was a poignant reminder that beauty and decay could coexist, that life's cycles were inescapable.

Her mind filled with curiosity, Amelia wondered about the significance of the throne, its purpose in this enigmatic room. It exuded a sense of importance, a silent invitation for someone to claim its seat of power and authority. But who was it meant for? And what role did it play in the grand scheme of their journey?

Lost in her thoughts, Amelia couldn't help but feel a mixture of reverence and nervousness in the presence of this enigmatic throne. It seemed to hold secrets yet to be revealed, mysteries waiting to be unraveled. As she stood before it, she couldn't shake the feeling that her next steps would be crucial, that her choices within this room would shape the course of their fate.

Amelia's attention was abruptly pulled away from the captivating sight of the throne as a powerful voice reverberated through the room, echoing with undeniable authority. It called out to her, piercing through the stillness that enveloped the chamber.

"Hello, child," the voice boomed with a slight feminine tinge, resonating with a commanding presence that demanded attention.

Startled, Amelia turned her gaze towards the source of the voice, her heart quickening with a mixture of anticipation and apprehension. She couldn't tell where the voice was coming from.

Amelia's heart pounded in her chest as she slowly walked backward, her gaze darting around the room, searching for the source of the mysterious voice. Her voice quivered with a mix of fear and curiosity as she called out, "Who's there?"

A moment of tense silence hung in the air, the only sound echoing through the chamber being the soft whisper of her own breath. Then, to her surprise, the voice responded, its tone calm and reassuring. "No one to fear, dear Amelia," it said, its words flowing through the air like a gentle breeze.

Amelia's brows furrowed in confusion as she tried to make sense of the enigmatic response. She cautiously glanced around, her senses on high alert. The room seemed devoid of any physical presence, yet the voice persisted, its ethereal quality tingling her senses.

Amelia's eyes widened in awe as she turned around in place, her gaze sweeping the room in search of the elusive voice. With each cautious step, her attention was drawn to the grand throne that occupied one side of the chamber. After a couple circles she stopped, and there, seated upon it, was a figure of majestic beauty.

Amelia's could not blink as she took in the appearance of the being on the throne. The stark contrast between its two sides was both striking and unsettling. The being wore a white cloak, its edges adorned with intricate golden patterns. On one side, the cloak flowed gracefully, pristine and untouched, radiating an aura of purity. But on the other side, it was stained, tattered, and falling apart, as if consumed by darkness and decay.

Her gaze shifted to the being's hands and feet, and the duality continued to captivate her attention. One hand was smooth, pale, and flawless, resembling the marble statues she had seen in museums. The other hand, however, revealed nothing but bone, stripped of flesh and vitality. The same contrast extended to its feet, with one side appearing ethereal and graceful, while the other side was skeletal and haunting.

Amelia couldn't help but feel a mixture of awe and unease as she observed the being before her. Its presence seemed to embody the delicate balance between light and darkness, life and death. It was a living paradox, a testament to the complexities of existence.

"I am the impartial observer of existence, the eternal companion on the journey from life to the unknown. I am the convergence of all destinies, the ultimate equalizer." Amelia stood in silence. "I am Death."

As Death spoke, its voice carried the weight of countless echoes, each a testament to the lives it had witnessed and guided. The words seemed to transcend time itself, a haunting reminder of the inevitable passage that awaits all beings.

With a slight, solemn head bow, Death acknowledged Amelia's presence. Its voice, filled with an ethereal resonance, cut through the stillness of the cosmic chamber.

Amelia took a step forward, her voice filled with a mix of anticipation and apprehension. "I am Amelia," she began, her voice soft but steady. "I am her to ask for your help."

Before she could continue, Death's voice resonated through the chamber, interrupting her introduction. "I know who you are, child," it spoke, the words carrying a weight that reverberated through Amelia's being. Its voice held an otherworldly knowledge, as if it had witnessed the passing of countless souls and the unfolding of myriad stories.

Amelia's annoyance flashed across her face, her brows furrowing slightly as she sought to assert her independence. "I am not a child," she stated, her voice tinged with a touch of defiance.

In response, Death's features remained impassive, its gaze piercing through her facade. "In the vastness of existence, child, you are but an infant. Mortality, fleeting as it may be, paints your existence with the hues of transience. Compared to the eternal dance of life and death, your steps are mere footprints in the sands of time."

Amelia's voice trembled slightly as she implored, "Please, I need your help."

Death regarded her with an enigmatic gaze, its presence casting an ethereal aura around them. A moment of silence hung in the air, pregnant with anticipation, as Amelia anxiously awaited a response. Finally, Death spoke, its voice carrying the weight of eternity. "Why should I help you, child?"

Amelia's voice trembled with a mix of frustration and anguish as she mustered the courage to confront Death. "I need your help to banish the Messenger," she implored, her voice quivering. "It was your doing, your fault in the first place, that the Messenger was able to torment and torment me."

Death regarded her with an inscrutable gaze, its presence exuding an otherworldly aura. A sigh escaped its spectral form, as if contemplating the weight of Amelia's accusation. "Why would I aid you in banishing the Messenger?" Death questioned, its voice laced with a hint of curiosity.

Amelia's eyes met the depths of Death's hallowed gaze, determination etched into her expression. "Because," she replied resolutely, "it was your own actions that set this chain of events in motion. By failing to banish the Messenger in the first place, you unknowingly subjected me to its torment. Now, I seek liberation, release from its malevolent grasp, and it is only fair that you assist me in undoing the consequences of your own intervention."

Silence filled the air, the weight of Amelia's words hanging between them. She could feel the gravity of the situation, the delicate balance between pleading and demanding. She knew that her fate hinged on Death's decision, and she held her breath, awaiting its response.

After a prolonged pause, Death's ethereal form shuddered with a deep, resonating laughter that seemed to echo throughout the chamber. Amelia felt a chill run down her spine as she absorbed the weight of Death's amusement. With a hint of incredulity, Death responded, "My doing, you say? Pray, do enlighten me, child. How is it that you attribute the blame to me?"

Amelia's mind raced, searching for a way to bridge the gap between the legend and her present reality. She recalled the words Isabella had shared, the tale of the music box,

Death's attempt at banishing the Messenger. It was a story passed down through generations, whispered in hushed tones, and etched into the tapestry of history.

Death, its enigmatic form fidgeting with a mix of curiosity and amusement, regarded Amelia with a detached air. "A beautiful story indeed," it responded, its voice tinged with a hint of wistfulness. "But stories are often nothing more than tales woven through time, embellished with each retelling."

Amelia's heart sank, her hopes deflated by the reality of Death's response. The legend that had offered solace and purpose now seemed nothing more than a fleeting dream. Doubt crept into her mind, threatening to overshadow her determination.

Death sat up, its form shifting and swirling with a newfound intensity, intrigued by her unwavering spirit. The air around them seemed to hold its breath as Death's voice resonated, cutting through the silence. "Would you like to know what really happened?" it asked, its tone carrying a mix of solemnity and curiosity.

Swallowing the lump in her throat, Amelia nodded slowly, her voice laced with uncertainty. "Yes," she replied, her voice barely above a whisper. "I want to know the truth."

Death's ethereal form seemed to flicker with a renewed intensity, as if anticipating this moment. With an air of quiet contemplation, it leaned forward, its eyes fixed on Amelia. "Very well," it responded, its voice carrying a weight of solemnity. "Prepare yourself, for the truth may be a burden you cannot easily bear."_

Chapter Nineteen
THE TRUTH BEHIND
THE TALE

Amelia stood frozen in the wake of Death's revelation, her mind swirling with a torrent of emotions. The weight of the truth crashed upon her like a tidal wave, shattering the delicate illusions she had clung to for solace. Reality, raw and unfiltered, pierced through the veil of her understanding, leaving her breathless and vulnerable.

"So, you created the Messenger out of boredom?" Amelia asked, her voice a fragile thread woven with sad curiosity.

Death nodded solemnly, its gaze, glinting through its shroud, fixed on Amelia. "Indeed, child," it replied, its voice carrying the weight of eons. "In the vast expanse of eternity, even Death can succumb to the throes of boredom. The Messenger, one of many my own creations, was an attempt to alleviate that weariness, a creation that soon spiraled out of control."

Amelia's mind reeled with the magnitude of Death's revelation. She tried to comprehend the implications of a force so ancient and powerful seeking solace through the creation of such a destructive entity. The realization that the very essence of Death was fallible, subject to the same yearnings and vulnerabilities as mortals, left her both awestruck and humbled.

"And after centuries of havoc, you tried to stop it?" Amelia questioned, her voice tinged with a mixture of sympathy and concern.

A somber expression crossed Death's features, its eyes reflecting the weight of untold battles fought and lost. "Indeed," it replied, its voice a whisper of remorse. "I attempted to put an end to the Messenger's rampage, but I soon discovered that I was unable to extinguish what I had birthed. The touch of death had imbued it with a resilience that even I could not overcome."

Amelia's heart sank as she grasped the magnitude of the situation. The Messenger, a being of chaos and torment, was beyond the reach of Death itself. She could feel the weight of the responsibility pressing upon her, the weight of being the agent of life in a world intertwined with death.

"So, only something born of life can stop the Messenger?" Amelia asked, her voice filled with a newfound sense of purpose.

Death nodded slowly, its gaze fixed intently upon Amelia. "Yes, only through the essence of life itself can the Messenger be vanquished," it confirmed. "You, Amelia, bear the spark of life within you, a power capable of quelling the Messenger's destructive force."

As Amelia stood there, absorbing Death's words, a feeling of awe washed over her. She watched as Death gracefully rose from the throne, its ethereal form gliding towards her. The air around them seemed to shimmer with an otherworldly energy.

"You see, Amelia," Death spoke, its voice carrying an air of both wisdom and sorrow. "I have long sought to contain the Messenger, to bring an end to its relentless reign of chaos. I trapped its essence within the music box and cast it into the mortal world, hoping that someone, someday, would arise with the power to conquer it."

Amelia's eyes widened with astonishment, her gaze fixed upon Death as it revealed the existence of the imprisoned Messenger. She could sense the gravity of the situation, the weight of the countless lives affected by the Messenger's malevolence.

"And you, Amelia," Death continued, its voice resonating with a profound sense of purpose, "have come the farthest of all. Through your resilience, your unwavering spirit, you have made it further than any who have attempted to face the Messenger before."

A mixture of pride and determination welled up within Amelia as Death pointed directly at her. The realization that she held the potential to bring about the Messenger's downfall, to end its reign of terror, filled her with a renewed sense of strength.

"But be warned, Amelia," Death cautioned, its voice filled with a solemn tone. "The path ahead will be treacherous, and the power of the Messenger is not to be underestimated. It will test your resolve, your very essence of being. Tell me, Amelia, will you do whatever is necessary to stop the Messenger?"

Amelia nodded, her eyes reflecting a look of determination. She understood the gravity of the task that lay before her, the enormity of the responsibility that had been placed upon her shoulders. Yet, she knew deep within her heart that she had come this far for a reason.

As Death's final words echoed through the chamber, it began to gradually recede, its ethereal form dissipating like mist. "Very well," Death's voice resonated one last time, filled with an enigmatic mix of determination and reassurance.

Amelia watched in awe as Death floated away, its presence becoming fainter with each passing moment. It gestured with a spectral arm, pointing towards one of the dimly lit corridors that stretched out before her.

Turning around, Amelia's gaze was met with the sight of a shadowy figure emerging from the depths of the corridor. It moved with an eerie grace, each step deliberate and filled with an air of mystery. The figure's silhouette danced along the walls, elongated and distorted by the flickering torchlight.

As Amelia's anticipation grew, the steps of the approaching figure echoed through the corridor, gradually growing louder and more distinct. The sound reverberated in her ears, building a sense of suspense. And then, stepping into the light, the figure revealed itself to be none other than Captain Styx, his weathered face etched with both relief and surprise.

"Captain Styx!" Amelia exclaimed, her voice filled with excitement and disbelief. She rushed toward him, a radiant smile illuminating her face, and threw her arms around him in a tight embrace. The captain, caught off guard by her sudden display of affection, hesitated for a moment before reciprocating the hug.

"Amelia," the captain said, his voice filled with a mix of astonishment and relief. "I can't believe it's really you. How did you...?"

Amelia pulled back slightly, her eyes shining with joy. "I made it through, Captain. I've come so far, and now I'm here to face the Messenger. I never gave up hope, and I knew you would be here to help."

Amelia's excitement gradually gave way to concern as she remembered her beloved brother, Milo. She pulled away from the captain's embrace, her eyes searching his face for answers.

"Captain Styx," she asked anxiously, "have you found Milo? Is he safe?"

The captain's expression softened with empathy as he met her worried gaze. "I'm sorry, Amelia. He's dead. I found his body while I was looking for you."

Amelia's face fell, a mixture of shock, grief, and disbelief washing over her features. She staggered back, as if the weight of the captain's words threatened to knock her off balance. "No... No, it can't be true," she whispered, her voice barely audible.

Amelia's mind was reeling from the devastating news of Milo's death, her thoughts consumed by grief and confusion. As she stood there, her body trembling with disbelief, the captain's question snapped her back to reality. She turned her gaze towards him, her eyes filled with a mix of shock and anger.

"How was it? How was it being in the presence of Death?" the captain asked, his voice filled with a hint of curiosity.

Amelia's expression contorted in disbelief, her voice quivering with a mixture of sadness and rage. "What? How can you ask me that? Milo is dead! He's gone, and all you care about is Death's presence? How can you be so callous?"

Amelia's heart sank as she watched the captain slowly pace around the room, his footsteps echoing in the chamber. A sense of fear gripped her, realizing that she had never shared with him the harrowing encounter she had with Death. She felt a knot tighten in her stomach.

Amelia mustered up the courage to speak, her voice quivering with trepidation. "Captain... how did you know about my meeting with Death? I never told you, so how do you know?"

The captain's footsteps abruptly halted, and a chuckle escaped his lips, breaking the seriousness of the moment. Amelia looked at him, puzzled by his sudden change in demeanor. "Captain, what's so amusing?"

The captain's laughter abruptly halted, and Amelia's heart skipped a beat as he turned around to face her. As he did, her breath caught in her throat, her eyes widening in shock and fear. Where his once vibrant and wise eyes had been, now resided an inky blackness that seemed to consume his very essence.

Amelia's voice trembled as she spoke, her words filled with both confusion and apprehension. "Captain... what... what happened to your eyes?"

The captain's voice cut through the air, dripping with malice and a twisted sense of satisfaction. "Don't break my heart, Amelia, and tell me you don't recognize me." His words were laced with a sinister undertone as he gave her a chilling smile, his eyes gleaming with a malevolent glint.

Amelia's heart sank, and fear coursed through her veins as the realization hit her like a thunderbolt. The pieces of the puzzle fell into place, and a name escaped her trembling lips. "Messenger," she whispered, her voice barely audible in the cavernous chamber, her eyes locked on the transformed captain.

The Messenger, its essence intertwined with the captain's form, reveled in its twisted victory. With a malevolent gleam in its eyes, it theatrically took a bow, a macabre display of triumph and malevolence. Its voice, distorted by the possession, echoed through the chamber, dripping with malice.

"Ladies and gentlemen," the Messenger's voice rang out, filled with a cruel delight, "allow me to present your demise, a performance like no other."

As it straightened up, the Messenger's presence loomed larger, casting a dark shadow over the chamber. Its twisted grin sent chills down Amelia's spine, a cruel reminder of the evil that now inhabited the captain's body.

Amelia's panic surged as she frantically scanned the room for an escape route. Her eyes darted from one corner to another, desperately seeking a glimmer of hope. With each passing moment, her fear intensified, fueling her desperate need for survival.

In a daring attempt to flee, Amelia mustered every ounce of strength and courage within her and lunged towards the captain, hoping to slip past his grasp. But the possessed body moved with an otherworldly speed, snatching her by the throat before she could even reach halfway.

Gasping for breath, Amelia found herself helplessly suspended in the air, her body now at the mercy of the

Messenger's grotesque puppet. The captain's once-familiar face contorted into a chilling visage, twisted by the malevolent force that held him captive.

As the Messenger tightened its grip, Amelia felt her body collide against the unforgiving wall with an alarming force. Pain radiated through her, threatening to consume her senses. Tears welled up in her eyes, mingling with the traces of fear that stained her cheeks.

The Messenger's voice, distorted and dripping with malice, seeped into Amelia's ears. "Do you truly believe you can escape, Amelia? Your futile attempts only amuse me. This is the dance we were destined to perform, and you will not escape its grip."

With an unnerving strength, the Messenger effortlessly hoisted Amelia off the ground, his grip unyielding and suffocating. Amelia struggled against his grasp, her body writhing in his clutches. In a malicious display of power, the Messenger flung her across the room, sending her hurtling through the air with a sickening force.

Amelia's body collided against the unforgiving surface, pain reverberating through her. As she landed with a thud, a sharp clatter echoed through the room. Unbeknownst to her, the concealed blade she had carried, a glimmer of hope in the face of darkness, had been dislodged from its hiding place during the chaotic upheaval.

The blade slid across the floor, its polished surface catching the dim light in a silent plea for attention. It came to a halt, nestled against a corner, waiting as if beckoning to be discovered.

Amelia gritted her teeth, determination mingling with the searing pain that radiated through her body. She fought against the throbbing ache, mustering every ounce of strength to rise to her feet. But before she could fully regain her footing, the Messenger, in a display of unnerving speed, was upon her, his presence overwhelming.

He loomed over Amelia, a twisted smirk etched across his face, taunting her with cruel words. "Is this all the fight you have, little mortal? I expected more from one who dares to challenge me."

Amelia's vision blurred as the Messenger's vice-like grip tightened around her throat. The room seemed to spin, and each gasp for breath became more desperate than the last. With her voice strained, she managed to choke out a plea, "Let... me go..."

The Messenger's eyes gleamed with sadistic delight as he exerted more pressure, relishing in Amelia's torment. His voice dripped with malevolence as he whispered, "You thought you could challenge me, but now you will learn the price of your defiance."

Amelia's struggles grew weaker as the world around her faded into darkness. The pain intensified, and her body grew limp under the Messenger's merciless grasp. In her final moments of consciousness, she looked around for anything to help her; fear took hold as she realized there was nothing.

As Amelia's life force ebbed away, time seemed to slow down, and her mind became a hazy kaleidoscope of memories. Images from her past flashed before her eyes, each one a testament to the joys, sorrows, and triumphs she had experienced. She saw the smile on Milo's face, the laughter they had shared, the moments of love and warmth with Carlos, and the short-lived adventure she shared with the captain, that had filled her heart.

But intertwined with those cherished memories were the moments of doubt and regret. The weight of her perceived failure settled upon her like a heavy shroud, engulfing her in a wave of self-doubt. She questioned if she had done enough, if she had truly fought with all her strength and will. A pang of guilt gripped her, as she wondered if she had let down those she cared about most.

Amelia's breath grew shallow, and her vision dimmed further, as the impending darkness closed in. Her heart ached with a deep sense of loss, the realization that her journey may have come to an untimely end. The bitter taste of failure lingered on her tongue, overwhelming her senses.

Amelia's consciousness flickered back to life, her senses gradually awakening from the depths of darkness. A piercing shriek reverberated through the chamber, rattling the very foundation of the ancient temple. Her vision blurred, but through the haze, she caught fleeting glimpses of the Messenger convulsing and thrashing about, desperately trying to grasp at something on its own back. A mixture of confusion and intrigue filled her mind as she struggled to make sense of the scene unfolding before her.

Amelia coughed, her body convulsing with the effort to regain control. Sitting upright, she rubbed her throat, feeling the lingering ache from the Messenger's grip. As she gathered her bearings, her eyes widened in astonishment at the sight before her.

There, standing face to face with the Messenger, was Milo. His expression was resolute, his gaze locked with the malevolent entity that had tormented them. The air crackled with tension as they stared each other down, an intense battle of wills playing out in their eyes.

With a sudden motion, the Messenger reached behind its back, a sinister smile curling upon its lips. Amelia's heart raced as she anticipated what the Messenger was about to reveal. And then, with a swift movement, it pulled a gleaming knife from its own back, its metallic glint casting an eerie shimmer in the dim light.

Amelia's breath caught in her throat as she watched the Messenger contemplate the blade for a brief moment before casually tossing it aside, the metallic clatter echoing through the chamber. A sense of confusion and curiosity mingled within her as she tried to grasp the meaning behind this unexpected action.

The fallen knife, its silver blade stained with blood from the captain's body, lay upon the cold stone floor. Its handle, a vibrant blue glass, shimmered in the dim light of the chamber.

Amelia focused her gaze on the knife, her curiosity guiding her closer. As she observed intently, a strange phenomenon unfolded. The blood on the blade seemed to defy logic, seeping into its metallic surface as if absorbed by an invisible force. But that was not all.

To Amelia's astonishment, the blood continued its journey, defying gravity, and began filling up the glass handle. The vibrant blue hue of the glass started to darken as the crimson liquid flowed within, creating intricate patterns and swirls, like a living canvas of the mysterious power it held.

Amelia crawled over and picked up the blade. She could feel its power as she held it in her hand, a sort of tingling. As stared curiously at the knife she noticed that the handle was still slightly empty.

It was then she remembered something Death had told her. *"Only through the essence of life itself can the Messenger be vanquished. You, Amelia, bear the spark of life within you, a power capable of quelling the Messenger's destructive force."*

Amelia, driven by an unyielding determination, held the knife firmly in her hand, feeling its weight and the cool touch of the blade against her palm. Without hesitation, she pressed the sharp edge against her skin, breaking through the delicate barrier and allowing her life's essence to flow forth.

As her palm bled, droplets of crimson fell onto the blade, each one absorbed by the steel with an insatiable hunger. The darkened handle, already brimming with the blood from before, eagerly embraced this new offering. The blade trembled with a newfound energy, its vibrations intensifying, while a low hum resonated through the air, permeating the chamber.

Amelia could sense the surge of power coursing through her veins, mingling with the ancient forces contained within the knife. The convergence of her life's essence and the enigmatic properties of the blade sparked a profound transformation, awakening a dormant magic that lay dormant within its core.

Amelia, her heart ablaze with a newfound power, rose from her place on the ground. Gripping the pulsating blade tightly, she fixed her gaze upon the scene unfolding before her. Milo, held captive against the wall by the Messenger, met her eyes with a silent understanding, a flicker of hope in his gaze.

Amelia took a step forward, her stance firm and resolute. The weight of the blade in her hand felt both familiar and foreign, a tangible extension of her determination. She could feel its energy coursing through her, empowering her with each passing moment.

With a steady breath, Amelia raised the blade, its silver edge glinting in the dim light. Her eyes locked onto the Messenger, its malevolent presence palpable in the air. The moment hung in suspended anticipation; the silence broken only by the faint hum emanating from the blade.

As the Messenger tightened its grip on Milo, a twisted smile contorted its face, relishing its moment of dominance. But Amelia would not be swayed by fear. With unwavering resolve, she prepared herself to confront this malevolent force, to protect those she cared for and defy the odds stacked against her.

In a voice laced with determination, Amelia called out to the Messenger, her words cutting through the charged atmosphere. "Your reign ends here!"

Chapter Twenty

Stabbed in the Back

Time seemed to stretch and bend to the rhythm of Amelia's determined heart. Every step she took echoed with purpose, each one a resolute beat propelling her forward. The world around her moved in slow motion, as if nature itself held its breath, anticipating the imminent clash between light and darkness.

Amelia's eyes blazed with an unwavering focus, fixated on the task at hand. In their depths, a storm of emotions churned—vengeance mingled with justice, sorrow intertwined with resolve. There was no room for doubt or hesitation. Her path was clear, her purpose resolute: to put an end to the Messenger's tyrannical reign and restore peace to her world.

"One swift and powerful motion," Amelia whispered, her voice laced with determination, as she lunged forward, the weight of the world behind her. The silver blade sliced through the air, finding its mark with unerring precision, piercing the Messenger's back. A guttural screech of pain erupted from the depths of the creature, reverberating through the ancient halls of the temple.

The Messenger momentarily released from its grip on Milo and staggered back, its once-imposing figure now hunched in agony. Eyes filled with fury locked onto Amelia, burning with an intensity that sent shivers down her spine. In that moment, she knew that she had roused the full wrath of the Messenger, and she braced herself for the impending battle.

With an enraged bellow, the Messenger unleashed a torrent of dark energy, its tendrils lashing out like serpents, seeking to ensnare and destroy. Amelia, undeterred, readied herself for an attack. The air crackled with tension as the forces of light and darkness clashed, an epic struggle unfolding before their eyes.

The Messenger, his voice dripping with venom, unleashed a torrent of anger and frustration as he closed in on Amelia. His steps were deliberate, each one punctuated by a furious proclamation.

"Foolish mortal," the Messenger sneered, his words laced with malice. "Did you really think you could challenge my power? You are nothing more than a fleeting spark, a mere insect in the grand tapestry of existence."

Amelia stood her ground, her eyes locked onto the approaching Messenger. Her face displayed a mix of determination and defiance as she prepared herself for the final confrontation.

"You may possess the illusion of strength," the Messenger continued, his voice carrying the weight of centuries of darkness. "But in the end, your feeble attempts will crumble before the might of my eternal reign. You cannot comprehend the depth of my power, the breadth of my dominion."

With every step, the Messenger's presence grew more imposing, his aura emanating a palpable malevolence that permeated the air. Shadows danced around him, a sinister symphony heralding his impending triumph.

Amelia's heart skipped a beat as the Messenger's sinister laughter filled the air, echoing through the chamber. His words hung heavy in the tense atmosphere, and a shiver ran down her spine. She tightened her grip on the dagger, her knuckles turning white, hoping that her weapon would prove enough to overcome this formidable adversary.

"You may have come this far," the Messenger sneered, his laughter lingering in the air like a malevolent echo. "But you remain ignorant of the one thing that could have won you this battle. You know not my name, the key to defeating me."

Amelia's mind raced, a mix of determination and apprehension clouding her thoughts. She had hoped that the dagger, infused with her own blood and the power of life, would be enough to vanquish the Messenger. But now, faced with his chilling revelation, doubt gnawed at her resolve.

The Messenger took a step closer, his eyes ablaze with a dark, unhinged intensity. Amelia could see the hunger for control in his gaze, the desire to keep his name concealed, a source of power and leverage over his opponents.

Milo's sudden intervention took both the Messenger and Amelia by surprise. With a burst of agility, he leaped onto the Messenger's back, his fingers gripping tightly onto the creature's sinewy shoulders. In a daring move, Milo leaned in close, his voice barely above a whisper, as if sharing a secret.

"She may not know your name," Milo began, his voice laced with an air of defiance, "but I do, Malachi. I know the very essence that defines you."

Amelia's eyes widened in astonishment, her heart racing with a mix of anticipation and curiosity. She had never expected Milo to possess such vital knowledge, to hold the key that could potentially turn the tide of their battle.

The Messenger, momentarily taken aback by Milo's audacity, froze in place. Its eyes widened in a mixture of fury and disbelief, realizing that the one person it had underestimated possessed the crucial information it sought to keep hidden.

As Milo's voice resonated with an otherworldly power, he spoke the Messenger's name, "Malachi," with unyielding resolve. With each syllable, the dagger in his hand seemed to vibrate, channeling his intention to bring about the Messenger's downfall. In a final act of defiance, Milo thrust the blade deeper into Malachi's back, piercing its malevolent heart.

A torrent of darkness erupted from Malachi's wound as the creature convulsed, its agonized shrieks piercing the air. Amelia's heart raced with a mixture of fear and relief as she witnessed the culmination of their struggle. The embodiment of darkness writhed and thrashed, its body contorting in a macabre dance of anguish and defeat.

Milo, weakened but resolute, crawled towards Amelia, his eyes locked onto hers. In that moment, their bond transcended words, an unspoken understanding passing between them.

With an outstretched hand, Amelia reached out to Milo, their fingers intertwining in a testament to their resilience.

Together, they bore witness to the demise of the Messenger, a manifestation of their collective strength and unyielding spirit.

Malachi's convulsions ceased abruptly, freezing in a twisted pose of agony. Its arms remained outstretched, its eyes fixated on the ceiling as if witnessing some unseen horror.

Black smoke billowed out from every orifice of Captain Styx's body, engulfing him in an ominous cloud. The air grew thick with the stench of decay and sulfur, and a low, guttural growl emanated from within the swirling darkness.

Amelia's heart raced, and she turned to face the haunting spectacle unfolding before her. Milo stood by her side, his expression a mix of concern and determination. The sludge-like substance seeped from Captain Styx's eyes, nose, mouth, and ears, oozing and dripping onto the cold stone floor.

"What... what is happening?" Amelia whispered, her voice trembling.

Milo's voice was steady, though tinged with caution. "It seems that the remnants of Malachi's presence within Captain Styx's body are being purged," he explained, his eyes fixed on the dark cloud enveloping their former companion.

The black smoke swirled and writhed, taking on grotesque forms that seemed to defy logic. Shadows twisted and contorted, creating grotesque faces and elongated limbs within the billowing mass. Amelia could feel a malevolent energy emanating from the smoke, a remnant of Malachi's essence desperately clinging to its host.

Suddenly, with a violent spasm, Captain Styx's body convulsed, and a final burst of black smoke erupted from him, dissipating into the air. The chamber fell silent once more, the oppressive presence lifted.

Amelia approached Captain Styx cautiously, her eyes filled with a mixture of sympathy and relief. "Captain?" she called, reaching out a trembling hand towards him.

Captain Styx's body slumped to the ground, lifeless and motionless. His eyes, once vibrant and full of life, were now dull and empty. The ordeal had taken its toll, and he had become a vessel for forces far beyond his control.

Amelia's heart sank as she heard Captain Styx's weak whisper. She hurriedly knelt beside him, cradling his head in her arms. Tears welled up in her eyes as she gazed into his weary face, realizing the gravity of his condition.

Captain Styx's voice was barely a whisper, but his smile remained unwavering. "Thank you, Amelia, for this final adventure," he murmured, his voice filled with gratitude and a sense of closure.

Amelia choked back a sob, her grip on his head tightening. "No, Captain, thank you for everything," she managed to say through her tears. "You've been a true friend and an inspiration to us all."

Captain Styx's eyes softened, and his voice grew weaker. "Remember, Amelia," he gasped, "it's the journey that defines us, not the destination. Cherish every moment."

Amelia nodded, her voice trembling. "I will, Captain. I promise."

In the midst of Captain Styx's final moments, a familiar presence emerged. Death, with a gentle smile, appeared by the captain's side. The room seemed to hush, enveloped in a solemn yet comforting atmosphere.

The captain's weary eyes met Death's serene gaze, a mixture of gratitude and acceptance reflected in his expression.

Death extended a hand, and without hesitation, the captain reached out, their hands intertwining in a gesture of trust and understanding.

With a voice filled with compassion, Death whispered, "It's time, Captain Styx. Your journey in this realm has come to an end, but fear not, for I shall guide you and reunite you with your beloved family."

A sense of peace washed over the captain's weary soul as he clung to Death's hand, relinquishing his earthly ties with a profound trust. In that moment, he felt the weight of his worries and sorrows lifted, replaced by the assurance of a joyful reunion beyond the veil.

With a final, contented sigh, Captain Styx's body went still. His smile lingered, frozen in time, etching the memory of his courage and selflessness into Amelia's heart.

Amelia and Milo watched in both awe and sorrow as Death led Captain Styx away, their figures fading into the ethereal glow that bathed the room. The solemnity of the moment resonated deeply within her, reminding her of the fragile nature of life and the eventual embrace of Death's gentle touch.

Milo's voice broke the silence that hung in the air, his tone laden with uncertainty and curiosity. "What do we do now?" he asked, his eyes searching Amelia's for answers.

Just as Amelia was about to respond, Death materialized before them once again. This time, however, there was a sense of camaraderie and accomplishment emanating from its presence. Death's voice, filled with a mixture of admiration and relief, spoke to the duo.

"Congratulations," Death said, its voice carrying a weight of sincerity. "You have succeeded in what I failed to do long ago. You have triumphed over the Messenger, and in doing so, you have shown resilience and strength beyond measure."

Amelia and Milo exchanged glances, their expressions a blend of surprise and awe at Death's unexpected words of praise. It was a validating moment, a recognition of their courage and tenacity in the face of unimaginable challenges.

Chapter Twenty-One

A LOVING MISTAKE

As Milo's curiosity led him to bombard Death with questions about the afterlife and the mysteries that lay beyond, Amelia's attention was momentarily diverted by a whisper that seemed to dance upon the air, calling her name. She turned her head, searching for the source of the faint but distinct voice.

"Amelia," the voice whispered once again, its timbre gentle yet persistent. Amelia's heart quickened with a mixture of anticipation and uncertainty. She felt a pull, an inexplicable longing to uncover the origin of the whispers that seemed to weave through the fabric of her being.

Excusing herself from the conversation between Milo and Death, Amelia followed the faint trail of the whispers, her steps guided by an invisible force.

Amelia's gaze shifted toward the dagger that lay in the corner of the room, its hilt adorned with a small, intricate key. There was an undeniable magnetism pulling her towards it, as if the dagger held the key to some hidden knowledge or path yet to be revealed. With a mix of curiosity and apprehension, Amelia extended her hand, slowly gripping the handle of the dagger.

As she lifted the dagger, a glimmer of light caught her eye, and Amelia's reflection shimmered upon the polished blade. But something was different this time. In the reflection, she saw a face she quickly recognized—the visage of Carlos, her lost love.

"Carlos?" Amelia whispered, her voice barely audible. She couldn't tear her eyes away from the reflection, captivated by the waves of emotions that surged within her.

The reflection of Carlos in the blade seemed to smile gently, his eyes filled with warmth and understanding. "Amelia, my love," his voice echoed in her mind, as if carried on a breeze from a distant memory. "It's time."

Milo's voice filled with excitement cut through the air. "Amelia, come quickly! What do you have there?" he called out, beckoning her over to where he stood. Curiosity piqued, Amelia turned toward him, her grip on the dagger tightening.

As Amelia prepared to respond, Death, ever watchful, turned its attention towards Amelia. Its eyes narrowed, a flicker of anger flashing across its features. "Where did you acquire that blade?" Death demanded, its voice laced with a mix of suspicion and annoyance.

Amelia hesitated for a moment, aware of Death's intensity. She looked from Milo to Death, and back to the dagger she held tightly. With a deep breath, she spoke cautiously, "I found it... in the temple. Carlos showed me."

Death's eyes bore into her, its gaze unyielding. "That blade carries a weight of ancient power, Amelia. It is not a tool to be taken lightly. The secrets it holds and the forces it can unleash are not to be trifled with. Hand it over," Death said, extending its arm.

As Death's demand hung in the air, Amelia reluctantly began to extend her hand, prepared to surrender the powerful blade. However, in that pivotal moment, a faint whisper reached her ears, a familiar voice. It was Carlos, his words barely audible yet filled with urgency. "Do not give Death the blade," he whispered, his voice resonating deep within Amelia's being.

Amelia's hand trembled, and a flicker of defiance sparked in her eyes. She hesitated, her gaze shifting between Death and the dagger in her grasp. A surge of determination coursed through her veins, fueled by the memory of Carlos and the unwavering trust they once shared.

Death's demand echoed through the chamber, its voice filled with stern authority. "Amelia, give me the blade," it commanded, its tone brooking no opposition.

But as Death's words hung in the air, Carlos leaned closer to Amelia, his voice a soft murmur in her ear. "Amelia, don't listen. Death is trying to keep us apart," he whispered, his words carrying a sense of urgency and caution.

Amelia's heart raced, torn between the weight of Death's command and the words of her beloved Carlos. She looked at Death, its imposing figure standing before her, and then turned her gaze back to the blade. The room seemed to hold its breath, caught in the tension of this pivotal moment.

Carlos's urgent whisper reverberated in Amelia's ear, his words carrying a desperate plea. "Amelia, if you give Death the blade, we will never be together," he warned, his voice filled with raw emotion.

Amelia's eyes widened with realization, and she clutched the blade tightly to her chest, feeling its cool metal against her skin. The weight of Carlos's words sank deep into her heart, fortifying her resolve. She couldn't bear the thought of a life without him, and she knew that surrendering the blade to Death would sever their connection forever.

As Amelia held the blade close, Death's anger erupted in a blazing inferno. The ethereal entity, consumed by fury, charged towards Amelia with an ominous presence. Its form seemed to distort, growing larger and more menacing with each passing moment.

As Death lunged toward Amelia, a sudden invisible barrier materialized before her, halting the menacing entity in its tracks. The ethereal figure recoiled, its face contorted with frustration and disbelief. In a voice filled with rage and curiosity, Death snarled, "What magic is this?"

Amelia, her heart pounding with a mixture of relief and awe, stared at the barrier that had materialized out of thin air. It shimmered with an otherworldly energy, pulsating with an indomitable power that seemed to repel Death's very essence.

Taking a step back, Death pressed its incorporeal form against the barrier, attempting to breach its defenses. But each attempt was met with resistance, the barrier holding strong against the onslaught. Frustration dripped from Death's voice as it exclaimed, "This should not be possible!"

Suddenly steps could be heard coming down one of the corridors. Curiously, Amelia, Death, and Milo stared at the corridor as a figure approached.

As the steps grew louder, echoing through the dimly lit corridor, a familiar figure emerged from the shadows. Carlos, with a smile that lit up the darkness, stepped into view. Amelia's heart leaped with joy, and she couldn't contain her excitement as she exclaimed, "Carlos!"

Milo's eyes widened in disbelief as he beheld Carlos standing before them. His voice trembled with a mixture of shock and awe as he spoke. "Carlos? Is that really you? How... how is this possible?"

Carlos turned his gaze towards Milo, a smile playing on his lips. His presence seemed to fill the space, radiating strength and determination. "Yes, Milo, it's me," he replied with unwavering certainty. "I have returned."

Death's expression twisted into a sneer, its eyes narrowing as it observed Carlos. "You," it spat, its voice dripping with contempt. "You dare stand in my presence?"

In a swift and decisive motion, Death lunged at Carlos, its malevolent energy propelling it forward. But Carlos, standing tall and resolute, lifted his hand, and an unseen force enveloped Death, freezing it in its tracks. With unwavering determination, he turned his gaze towards Amelia, their eyes locked in a moment of shared understanding.

"Amelia," Carlos spoke with a sense of urgency, his voice tinged with the weight of their predicament. "I can only hold Death for a limited time. You must take the blade and strike its heart."

Amelia's heart raced as she absorbed Carlos's words, the gravity of the situation weighing heavily upon her. She glanced at the blade in her hand, its gleaming edge and vibrant gold hilt seeming to pulsate with a power she had yet to fully comprehend. With each passing moment, the burden of the task ahead became more apparent.

Carlos continued, his voice a mix of unwavering determination and underlying concern. "You possess the strength, Amelia. You must pierce Death's heart with the blade. It is the only way to break its hold over us."

Amelia's breath caught in her throat as she internalized the enormity of the responsibility thrust upon her. She looked into Carlos's eyes, seeing the unwavering belief and trust he held in her. With a resolute nod, she steeled herself for the inevitable confrontation.

Taking a deep breath, Amelia moved closer to the restrained form of Death. The air crackled with tension as she raised the blade, its pulsating energy resonating with her own. She felt a surge of courage welling up within her, bolstered by the love and support of Carlos.

Milo's senses heightened, his intuition alerting him to an impending danger. With urgency in his eyes he walked towards Amelia, intent on warning her. However, before he could utter a single word, Carlos, ever perceptive, recognized the impending threat. With a swift motion and a whispered incantation, Carlos conjured a binding spell, sealing Milo's mouth shut.

Milo's eyes widened in surprise, his attempts to speak futile. He looked at Carlos, a mixture of confusion and frustration etched across his face. Though unable to voice his concerns, his eyes pleaded for Carlos to reconsider, to allow him to warn Amelia. Carlos, however, stood resolute, the weight of their precarious situation evident in his gaze.

Amelia, oblivious to the unfolding scene, stood firm, her focus solely on the task at hand. The blade still clutched tightly in her hand, she prepared herself to confront Death, unaware of Milo's silenced plea. The air crackled with tension as she took a step forward, ready to strike the final blow.

The air thickened with tension as Amelia stood face to face with Death, the weight of their confrontation palpable. Death, its gaze unyielding, fixed its eyes upon her. It spoke with a voice that echoed through the depths of despair, seeking to undermine her resolve.

"Amelia, you must understand," Death began, its tone dripping with a calculated charm. "Carlos is not who you think he is. He is but an illusion, a puppet in a grand scheme."

Carlos, his voice laced with urgency and determination, called out to Amelia, his words punctuating the air. "Amelia, don't listen to Death! It will say anything to manipulate you, to preserve its own existence."

Amelia's heart wavered, caught between the persuasive allure of Death's words and the steadfast conviction in Carlos's voice. Confusion knitted her brow as she tried to discern the truth amidst the chaos.

Death, sensing the internal struggle within Amelia, continued its assault on her resolve. "You cannot trust the illusions it conjures. I am the embodiment of truth, and I assure you, Carlos is not what he appears to be."

Carlos, undeterred by Death's attempts to sow doubt, raised his voice even louder, the urgency in his words cutting through the uncertainty. "Amelia, remember our bond, our shared experiences. Trust in our connection. Do not allow Death to twist the truth."

Amelia's eyes darted back and forth between Death and Carlos, a battle raging within her. Her mind raced, searching for a way to discern the truth, to unravel the intricate web of deception woven before her.

In that moment, her gaze locked with Carlos, and the depth of their connection ignited a spark of clarity within her. She found solace in the unwavering trust they had built, and the flicker of doubt within her began to fade.

Taking a deep breath, Amelia braced herself, her voice rising above the clamor. "I will not be swayed by your words, Death. Carlos has shown me his loyalty, his love. I choose to believe in the bond we share. I love him."

Amelia, driven by determination and a glimmer of hope, summoned every ounce of strength within her and thrust the blade deep into Death's chest. A bone-chilling scream erupted from Death's lips, reverberating through the walls of the temple. The ground beneath them quaked as the immense power contained within Death began to stir.

As Death convulsed, its body lifted off the ground. The room trembled violently, ancient stones crumbling under the sheer force of Death's awakening. Amelia, her eyes wide with both awe and fear, released her grip on the blade, her hands trembling as she took a step back.

But before she could distance herself from the malevolent entity, Death's hands shot out, gripping her wrists with an icy grip that sent shivers down her spine. The air grew heavy with an oppressive darkness, suffocating her senses. Death's face contorted with a mix of agony and fury, its eyes fixated on Amelia, burning with a twisted desire for retribution.

"Amelia," Death hissed, its voice a chilling whisper that seemed to echo from the depths of the underworld. Death's grip burned into Amelia's flesh; she screamed. When Death finally let her go, she fell to the ground. Amelia looked at her wrists and gasped, Death's grip permanently scarred on her, a form of cosmic restraints.

With a surge of urgency, Milo rushed to Amelia's side, his hand gripping hers tightly as they watched the unfolding spectacle before them. Death's attention diverted to the glowing blade lodged within its chest. A shimmering radiance emanated from the blade, growing brighter with each passing second.

Amelia's gaze fixated on the hilt, which detached from the blade, transforming into a key of radiant energy. It floated mid-air, suspended by an unseen force. The air crackled with an otherworldly energy, anticipation hanging thickly in the atmosphere.

The key descended gracefully to the floor, causing the ground to tremble softly upon contact. In an ethereal display of magic, a music box materialized before Amelia and Milo's eyes, its intricate design bathed in an otherworldly glow. The key found its rightful place in the lock, turning with a gentle click that resonated through the air.

As the lid of the music box slowly opened, a brilliant and blinding light spilled forth, casting a radiant glow upon the surroundings. The light grew in intensity, illuminating the chamber with a divine brilliance that banished the shadows of despair.

With a powerful suction, Death, unable to resist the irresistible pull, was inexorably drawn towards the open music box. Its form began to dissolve, fragments of darkness swirling and contorting as they were forcibly pulled into the captivating abyss. Amelia and Milo watched in awe as Death, once a formidable presence, was consumed by the enchantment of the music box.

The music box's lid closed with a resounding click, a shockwave moving throughout the entirety of the earth's surface, sealing Death's essence within its confines. The chamber fell into a tranquil silence, the weight of Death's existence vanquished. However, the respite was short-lived as the key shattered into three distinct pieces, each fragment flying away breaking through the confines of the ceiling, and the temple starts to collapse around Amelia and Milo.

Amidst the chaos and the deafening rumble of the collapsing temple, Amelia cast a fleeting glance towards Carlos, who stood there with a sinister smile. Before she could react, he vanished into thin air, leaving her with a lingering sense of unease. Milo's urgent voice broke through the turmoil, pulling her back into the present moment.

"Amelia, we need to go! Now!" Milo's voice echoed with urgency as he grabbed her hand, their fingers intertwining tightly as Amelia quickly picked up the music box. With determination in his eyes, he guided her through the crumbling corridors of the temple, their footsteps echoing against the crumbling walls.

As debris fell around them, dust filled the air, making it difficult to see. Amelia's mind raced, filled with doubts and questions. She couldn't help but wonder if she had made the right choice, if plunging the blade into Death's chest had truly brought about the desired outcome. The weight of responsibility pressed upon her, threatening to overshadow her confidence.

Milo swiftly guided Amelia through the labyrinthine corridors of the crumbling temple, their every step a dance of survival. Above them, chunks of stone and debris rained down, threatening to impede their progress.

With each agile dodge and nimble maneuver, they managed to navigate through the treacherous maze of falling rubble. The air was thick with dust, making it difficult to breathe, but the distant glow of daylight at the entrance offered a glimmer of hope. It beckoned them forward, promising safety and freedom from the crumbling confines.

Milo's voice echoed through the chaos, filled with both reassurance and exhilaration. "We're almost there, Amelia! Keep going! We can make it!" His words fueled Amelia's determination, her heart pounding in her chest as she pushed herself to keep up the pace.

Their bodies moved as one, their footsteps a synchronized rhythm amidst the disarray. The path ahead seemed never-ending, obstacles arising at every turn, but they pressed on, fueled by the unwavering belief that their escape was within reach.

And then, as if guided by a benevolent force, they broke through the final barrier. Sunlight poured in, bathing them in its warm embrace, as they stumbled out of the collapsing temple into the open air. Amelia gasped for breath, her lungs filling with the refreshing scent of freedom.

Milo, standing by her side, took a moment to catch his breath before turning to her with a triumphant grin. "We did it, Amelia! We made it out!"

Relief washed over her, mingled with a sense of accomplishment. She nodded, a mix of gratitude and exhaustion evident in her voice. "Thank you, Milo. I couldn't have done it without you."

As they stood on the precipice of the temple's ruins, they gazed back at the wreckage, a testament to the trials they had overcome. The light of the outside world embraced them, as if congratulating their resilience and determination.

Amelia and Milo stood in awe as they watched the aftermath of the temple's collapse. The once-majestic structure now lay in ruins, its remnants scattered across the ground. Dust and debris hung in the air, shimmering in the sunlight that broke through the clouds.

But their attention was soon drawn to a terrifying sight. From the heart of the wreckage, thirteen dark, sinuous trails of black smoke emerged, swirling and writhing like ethereal serpents. Each trail coiled and twisted, gaining momentum before shooting off into the distance, disappearing into the horizon.

Amelia's voice trembled. "What were those, Milo? Where did they come from?"

Milo's eyes widened with realization as he watched the trails vanish. "I... I'm not entirely sure, Amelia. But I have a feeling those trails have something to do with Death being trapped within the music box."

Amelia and Milo made their way back to the beach in solemn silence. Each step felt heavy, burdened by the weight of the recent events they had endured.

As they walked side by side, their minds filled with the remnants of their harrowing journey, their eyes occasionally met, conveying an unspoken understanding. Amelia's gaze would drift to the scars on her wrists, a stark reminder of the encounter with Death, the indelible marks left behind as a testament to her survival.

The scars served as a constant reminder of the darkness they had faced, the moments when their lives hung in the balance, and the ultimate triumph over the forces that sought to consume them. It was a visible reminder of the strength they had discovered within themselves and the resilience that had brought them through the depths of despair.

Amelia longed to speak, to find solace in sharing her thoughts and emotions with Milo. Yet, the weight of their experiences seemed to stifle their words, leaving them both lost in their own reflections.

They continued their journey in silence, the gentle rhythm of their footsteps creating a sense of companionship even without words. It was a silent understanding, a mutual acknowledgment of the pain they had endured and the unspoken support they offered each other.

As they reached the beach, the sand beneath their feet felt both familiar and foreign. The vast expanse of the ocean stretched out before them, its waves whispering stories of both beauty and turmoil. Amelia took a deep breath, allowing the sea breeze to fill her lungs, cleansing her of the residual darkness that clung to her.

Milo's eyes widened as he spotted a small boat pulled up on the beach, seemingly waiting for them. With a surge of hope, he rushed over to a group of men standing near the boat, their faces weathered by time and experience. Desperation filled his voice as he implored, "Please, we need your help. Can you take us away from this place?"

The men exchanged glances, their curiosity piqued by the urgency in Milo's plea. After a brief moment of deliberation, one of them nodded and said, "Aye, lad, we can take you wherever you need to go. Hop on board."

Milo's eyes sparkled with relief as he gestured for Amelia to join him. "Amelia, come quickly! These kind men have offered to help us. We're finally getting out of here."

Amelia, her heart filled with a mix of gratitude and dismay, hurried over to join Milo and the men. The sight of the boat bobbing gently in the water seemed like a lifeline, a tangible escape from the trials they had endured. With a renewed sense of hope, she stepped onto the vessel, feeling the wooden planks beneath her feet.

As they pushed off from the shore, the rhythmic sound of oars dipping into the water filled the air. Amelia couldn't help but steal a glance back at the fading silhouette of the beach, the place that held both darkness and moments of triumph. A bittersweet mixture of emotions swelled within her, but she couldn't shake the feeling that something evil lurked on the horizon._

Chapter Twenty-Two
MELANCHOLY PEACE

A couple of years had passed since Amelia's escape from the clutches of darkness, and she found solace in the tranquil town of Rincón del Olvido in Spain. Nestled along the sun-kissed coastline, the picturesque village had become her haven, a place where she could heal and rebuild her life.

As Amelia strolled through the cobblestone streets, the warmth of the Mediterranean sun caressed her skin, casting a golden glow upon the whitewashed buildings adorned with vibrant bougainvillea. The salty breeze carried the fragrance of the sea, mingling with the sweet scent of orange blossoms, enveloping her senses.

Amelia had embraced the slower pace of life in the town, immersing herself in the rich culture and warmth of the locals. She had found comfort in the rhythmic ebb and flow of daily routines, the vibrant conversations that filled the air, and the mouthwatering aromas wafting from the local tapas bars.

Amelia and Milo's bond had only deepened over the years, becoming a steadfast friendship that weathered the tests of time. They remained inseparable, supporting each other through life's triumphs and challenges. However, while Milo had found love and built a family, Amelia's heart remained haunted by the memory of Carlos, the one she had lost.

Milo, having found his own place of solace and belonging, settled down in Isabella's old home. With dedication and care, he lovingly restored the once-abandoned church that had provided sanctuary to both him and Amelia during their perilous journey. Through long hours of meticulous work, the worn walls were rejuvenated, and the ancient stained-glass windows once again dazzled with vibrant colors.

She watched with a mixture of joy and bittersweet longing as Milo found his soulmate in the enchanting Katrina. Together, they embarked on their own journey, building a life filled with love and laughter. Amelia witnessed their love story unfold, cherishing their happiness while quietly yearning for her own lost love.

As Milo and Katrina's family grew, Amelia played a cherished role in the lives of their children. She became the beloved aunt, sharing stories of their father's daring adventures, igniting their imaginations with tales of bravery and wonder. Amelia's presence in their lives brought joy and a touch of magic, as she imparted the lessons she had learned from her own extraordinary experiences.

But deep within her heart, Amelia carried the torch of love for Carlos, a flame that refused to be extinguished. She held onto his memory, treasuring the moments they had shared, and carrying the weight of the love that had transcended time and space.

Amidst the laughter and joy that surrounded her, there was a part of Amelia that remained guarded, shielding herself from the vulnerability of opening her heart to another man. Carlos had left an indelible mark, a love that had transcended the physical realm, and Amelia feared that by allowing another man to enter her heart, she would somehow betray the love they had shared.

Yet, as she watched Milo and Katrina's love blossom and witnessed the profound bond they shared, Amelia couldn't help but feel a sense of hope. Seeing the happiness they had found, she realized that love had the power to heal, to mend the deepest wounds, and to offer the possibility of new beginnings.

Amelia, with the support of Milo and his loving family, found herself the proud owner of the old library that had stood for generations. The wooden doors creaked as she entered, the scent of aged books and knowledge enveloping her with a comforting embrace. The shelves, once dusty and neglected, now held rows upon rows of meticulously organized volumes, each containing stories waiting to be discovered.

With a sense of purpose and passion, Amelia immersed herself in the world of literature, spending countless hours within the walls of the library. It became her sanctuary, a place where her curiosity thrived, and her imagination soared. She explored the realms of history, science, fiction, and poetry, losing herself in the words that danced across the pages.

Milo and his family, recognizing Amelia's deep connection to the library, stood by her side, offering their unwavering support. Milo's voice echoed through the stacks of books as he shared tales with his own children, passing down the love for storytelling that he had cultivated alongside Amelia.

Amelia, surrounded by the treasures of knowledge, often found solace in the quiet moments spent amidst the hallowed halls of the library. It became her haven, a place where she could reflect, dream, and find inspiration for her own writings. She would sit at an old oak desk, her pen gliding across parchment as she poured her thoughts onto paper, creating stories that blended reality and imagination.

Visitors came from near and far, drawn to the charm and warmth that emanated from the library. Amelia, always eager to share her love for literature, would engage in conversations with kindred spirits, guiding them through the vast collection of books, offering recommendations, and fostering a sense of community within the walls she had come to call her own.

As Amelia roamed the aisles, her fingers grazing the spines of beloved classics, she often thought of the journey that had brought her here, from the darkness of the past to the light of her present. She recognized the power of books to heal, to ignite a spark of hope, and to shape the lives of those who embraced them.

In the library's embrace, Amelia found fulfillment and purpose. With each passing day, she continued to write her own story, not only through her literary creations but also through the connections she forged with fellow book lovers and the legacy she nurtured within the walls of the old library.

As the years unfolded, an unsettling truth began to surface: Amelia, despite the passage of time, remained untouched by the grasp of aging. It was a peculiar anomaly that defied logic and left her pondering the reasons behind such a phenomenon.

Amelia, burdened by the weight of her immortality, found solace in the embrace of Milo's family, who had become her steadfast confidants. They, too, carried the secret of her unchanging visage, guarding it like a precious treasure hidden within the depths of their hearts.

Thoughts of curiosity and speculation swirled around Amelia's mind, like elusive whispers in the wind. Some whispered that it was a cruel jest played by fate, a never-ending reminder of her connection to the realm of Death. Others pondered if it was a form of divine punishment, a consequence for the entanglement that had unfolded in the depths of the ancient temple.

The townsfolk began to notice. Whispers spread through the town, murmurs of curiosity and speculation.

Amidst the hushed conversations and lingering glances, Milo's family remained loyal, protecting Amelia's secret from prying eyes. They shielded her from the scrutiny of the world, understanding the weight of the burden she carried. In their eyes, she was not an oddity to be gawked at but a cherished friend who had endured more than anyone should.

Time continued its relentless march, and eventually, in what felt like a mere blink of an eye for Amelia, Milo's journey in this world came to a close. The weight of his absence settled heavily upon her heart, a profound sense of loss and sorrow consuming her.

As the townspeople gathered to pay their respects, Amelia stood at the edge of the somber gathering, her eyes fixated on the coffin that held her dear friend. Memories flooded her mind, each one etched with the indelible mark of their shared adventures and unwavering bond.

"I'll miss you, Milo," Amelia whispered softly, her voice carrying the weight of a lifetime of memories. "You were there with me through it all, and I can't imagine this world without you."

The wind whispered through the ancient trees, rustling the leaves as if in response. Amelia knew that life was a delicate tapestry, woven with the threads of joy and sorrow, love and loss. And in that moment, she realized that even with her eternal existence, the pain of parting was an indelible part of the human experience.

With a heavy heart and a sense of longing, Amelia made the decision to embark on a journey that would take her far from the familiar streets of Rincón del Olvido. The weight of grief for Milo's passing hung heavily upon her, urging her to seek solace in new horizons and unfamiliar lands.

As she packed her belongings and prepared for the unknown, Amelia shared a heartfelt conversation with Milo's children and grandchildren, who now held the responsibility of the cherished library. With a mix of sorrow and hope in her voice, she spoke softly to them, her words carrying the weight of a promise.

"I entrust the library to you, my dear ones," Amelia said, her eyes filled with both nostalgia and anticipation. "It holds the stories and knowledge of generations, and I have faith that you will continue to nurture its legacy. I will return one day, for the library is a part of my soul, but for now, I must seek solace beyond these walls."

Milo's children and grandchildren, their faces reflecting the echoes of their beloved ancestor, nodded solemnly, understanding the depth of Amelia's connection to the library. They knew that in her absence, they would become the guardians of not just the physical space but the memories and wisdom it held.

Amelia took a lingering look at the library, its shelves filled with books whispering the tales of countless lives and untold adventures. She knew that within those hallowed walls, Milo's spirit would continue to reside, forever woven into the fabric of their shared history.

With a final farewell, Amelia set off on her journey, her footsteps carrying her away from the town that had been her sanctuary for so long. As the road stretched out before her, she felt a mix of trepidation and anticipation, the allure of the unknown beckoning her onward.

Days turned into weeks, and weeks into months as Amelia wandered through distant lands, immersing herself in new cultures, and encountering diverse souls along the way. Each step brought a semblance of healing, a gradual mending of the heart that had been shattered by loss.

Throughout her travels, Amelia found solace in the embrace of nature's beauty, seeking solace in the grandeur of mountains, the serenity of lakes, and the whispers of ancient forests. In these moments, she felt a connection to something greater than herself, a reminder that life's vast tapestry extends far beyond the boundaries of a single town or a single lifetime.

As the years passed, Amelia's adventures became etched in the lines on her face, a testament to the richness of her experiences. She carried within her the stories of the places she had visited, the people she had encountered, and the lessons she had learned along the way.

And though her absence was felt deeply in Rincón del Olvido, the library continued to flourish under the care of Milo's descendants. They honored their promise to Amelia, ensuring that the doors remained open to those seeking knowledge and inspiration.

As the winds of change whispered in her ear, Amelia knew that the time would come for her to return to the embrace of her cherished library and the familiar streets of Rincón del Olvido. But for now, she allowed the world to guide her, embracing the ebb and flow of life's currents, knowing that every step taken was a step closer to healing and growth.

As the years stretched into decades and the echoes of Amelia's departure faded from memory, the legend of her existence grew within the hearts and minds of the inhabitants of Rincón del Olvido. Her name became synonymous with courage, wisdom, and the boundless pursuit of knowledge. Tales of her adventures and her unwavering spirit were passed down through the generations, engraving her legacy into the very fabric of the town's history.

When Amelia finally returned to her beloved library, the weight of time and solitude lifted from her shoulders, replaced by a bittersweet blend of nostalgia and awe. As she stepped through the familiar doors, the air seemed to hold a whisper of recognition, as if the very walls and books welcomed her home.

Within the library's hallowed halls, Amelia found herself surrounded by faces she had never met, yet who knew her intimately through the tales of her exploits. The descendants of Milo's children and grandchildren stood before her, their eyes shining with reverence and a sense of connection that transcended the boundaries of time.

"It is you," they murmured, their voices carrying the echoes of the past. "The one who journeyed far and wide, whose name has become the fabric of our heritage. Welcome home, Amelia."

Amelia's heart swelled with a mix of emotions, a blend of gratitude and humility. She had left a town grieving for the loss of her presence but had returned to a town that revered her memory. In that moment, she understood the profound impact her life had made on Rincón del Olvido, how her legacy had become intertwined with the very essence of the town itself.

During one beautiful sunset, as the golden rays of the dying sun painted the library in warm hues, Amelia meticulously tidied up the scattered books and gently placed them back on the shelves. The day had been filled with visitors eager to explore the vast expanse of knowledge the library offered, and now it was time to bid them farewell.

As she diligently went about her tasks, the soft creak of the front door caught Amelia's attention. She turned, her eyes searching the shadowy entrance of the library. With a warm smile, she called out, her voice carrying through the silent aisles, "We're closing, but feel free to take a look around."

The stranger's eyes danced with admiration as they surveyed the expansive collection of books that adorned the library's shelves. "What a remarkable collection you have here," they exclaimed, their voice filled with genuine appreciation. "It is clear that this library has been nurtured and cherished over the years."

Amelia's smile widened, her heart swelling with pride for the labor of love that the library represented. "Thank you," she replied warmly, her voice tinged with a hint of nostalgia. "This collection is indeed a treasure, one that has grown and flourished through the passing of generations."

Amelia's footsteps echoed softly against the polished wooden floor as she made her way back to the front of the library. She cast a warm smile at the stranger who had entered, their features shrouded by the play of shadows. "Is there something specific that I can help you find?" she inquired, her voice filled with genuine curiosity.

As if guided by an invisible force, the stranger stepped forward, their face slowly emerging from the veil of darkness. A gentle smile curled their lips, revealing a glimmer of familiarity. "I believe you can," they replied, their voice holding a hint of familiarity that tugged at Amelia's memories.

Amelia stood there, her heart pounding within her chest, her voice caught in her throat. The weight of emotions swirled within her, rendering her momentarily speechless. With a gentle smile, the stranger broke the silence. "It's good to see you again, Amelia," they said, their voice filled with a calm sincerity.

The word escaped Amelia's lips in a breathless whisper, encapsulating the flood of emotions that surged through her. It was a simple word, yet it carried with it a depth of meaning that words alone could not convey. The years of longing, the memories etched deep within her heart, all culminated in that single utterance. "You."